Kenya
I speak the Blessing
And Favor of God
your ministry and
God is faithful to
your labor of Love

Juliette Alston

THE
Ugly Duckling
SYNDROME

JULIETTE ALSTON

Scriptures taken from King James Version
Copyright ©2004 by Thomas Nelson, Inc.

Scripture taken from The Holy Bible, New International Version.
Copyright 1973,1978,1984 International Bible society. Used by permission
Of Zondervan Bible Publishers

ISBN 978-0-9834895-1-1

CONTENTS

Dedication vii

A Love Letter to My Family ix

Introduction xi

Fairy Tales, Fantasy Tales, and Fantastic Tales xiii

Chapter 1 The Ugly Duckling Syndrome 1

Chapter 2 Honor thy Father and Mother........................ 17

Chapter 3 Trusting God 27

Chapter 4 Sleeping Beauty Syndrome 31

Chapter 5 The Emperor's New Clothes 39

Chapter 6 Rapunzel Syndrome......................................51

Chapter 7 The Cinderella Syndrome 59

Chapter 8 Jack and the Magic Beans 67

Chapter 9 Goldilocks 77

Chapter 10 The Princess and the Frog.............................85

Chapter 11 Beauty and the Beast 93

Chapter 12 The Boy Who Cried Wolf............................ 101

Chapter 13 The Three Little Pigs 107

Chapter 14 The Grasshopper and the Ant...................... 113

Chapter 15 Fascinating Tales..123

Epilogue 133

Notes 137

DEDICATION

This book is dedicated to everyone who has struggled with self-image regardless of whether you were aware of it or not. I was only made aware of my struggle because of the need for someone else to overcome the challenges that were hindering their spiritual growth. Thanks to my wonderful husband who has always affirmed, encouraged and supported me through my ugly duckling stage and now my beautiful swan stage. I love you, honey.

To Pastor Carolyn Spellman:

You have been critically instrumental in my spiritual growth. Thank you for looking beyond the shy, timid duck creature and seeing me in a delivered state as a beautiful swan. I can't express what I feel about your dedication to the Lord to bring His people into a place of total surrender to God. By now you know that your labor isn't in vain. I love you tremendously.

Forever grateful,
Juliette

A LOVE LETTER TO MY FAMILY

Dearest Family,

I love you with the love of the Lord. God has sent me to preserve posterity in the earth for you. He has taken what the enemy meant for evil and turned it around for our good. We were created in His image, so therefore whenever you lose hope or lose your way on the path to destiny, all you have to do is to look in the mirror of His word. It'll reflect His image, and lead you on the path of righteousness. I believe with every fiber of my being that we're destined for greatness. We aren't ugly ducklings but beautiful swans. We aren't bad actors. God said everything He created is good. We aren't less than but more than conquerors. We were fearfully and wonderfully made, created for His glory; therefore, we'll be translated out of darkness into the marvelous light. We'll see the Creator before He opens and closes the book on our stories. I love you.

Truly yours in Christ,
Juliette

INTRODUCTION

My experience as a child birthed this book. My fantasyland sustained me during long lonely days and fearful, terrifying nights. I'm not alone in this story. Those who read it and receive healing will understand the process. I'm writing to my biological family as well as those related by the new birth. I want to say to those who need a word of truth and encouragement: I love you with the love of the Lord. You were created for the glory of the Lord, and I pray that one day you'll look into the mirror and see yourself as He sees you. There aren't ugly ducklings in the kingdom.

I spent so much time reading fairy tales during my childhood and teenage years that God chose to allow me to tell my story of deliverance through the vehicle of a fairy tale. I now know that fairy tales aren't true, but I also understand that some truths may be extracted from them. The fact is that I'm no longer in bondage from the memories of my past. I'm only free by the grace of God. He changed my story before I was allowed to tell it. God wouldn't have gotten the glory if I hadn't triumphed in life after all of the struggles.

The ending of my story may be the beginning of someone else's story. You have to be able to distinguish a fairy tale from reality; otherwise, you may get stuck in fantasyland. Once upon a time and the present are completely different. I'll also tell the story of some of the readers of this book, and I'll do it in a way that is real to me. You'll know your account when you read it. You may experience emotions that have buried themselves within your memories, but I urge you to allow them to surface so that you may heal and be free of the pain. My heart is with you on this journey as I relive my story and yours narrated by God.

Love,
Juliette

FAIRY TALES, FANTASY TALES, AND FANTASTIC TALES

A fairy tale is a story, often intended for children, that features fanciful and wondrous characters such as elves, goblins, and even wizards, but not necessarily, fairies. The term "fairy" tale seems to refer more to the fantastic and magical setting or magical influences within a story, rather than the presence of the character of a fairy within that story. Fairy tales are often traditional; many were passed down from storyteller to storyteller before being recorded in books. Fairy tales are important because they spark the imagination. They give us an outlet for experiencing things in our minds before we experience them in the real world. It is where the troubles of the real world can meet the supernatural and mix things up. In a fairy tale, anything can happen, any kind of creature can exist, and when anything can happen, we can find solutions to things in our real lives. Through imagination, we learn about our world. We can explore the outcomes and possibilities.

Fantasy Tales: Fantasy; imagination, especially when extravagant and unrestrained. The forming of mental images, especially wondrous or strange fancies; imaginative conceptualizing.

Tale: a narrative that relates the details of some real or imaginary event, incident, or case; story:

Fascinating Tales

I find the stories in the Bible to be so fascinating that I can read them over and over without getting bored or tired of them. In this book, you'll find Bible characters that correspond with the characters in fairy tales. I was able to imagine the characters and their mannerisms and compare them to each other. I studied the places and circumstances in which the authors wrote their material. I placed myself in the stories as an interested observer and wondered what would have happened if they were in another time or place. I immersed myself in the stories and loved every minute of it. I believe the Bible to be infallible and that is why I think it is so fascinating.

CHAPTER ONE

The Ugly Duckling Syndrome

2 Corinthians 3:18

But we all, with open face beholding as in a glass the glory of the Lord, are changed into the same image from glory to glory, even as by the Spirit of the Lord.

There are times when we wonder how others perceive us, and there are even times when we contemplate who we are and what is our purpose. I won't pretend to know those answers for others; however, I'll share what I know for myself. I know without a shadow of a doubt that I'm created in the image of the God who created Heaven, Earth and everything and everybody in between. I know that I'm being transformed from glory to glory by the word and the Spirit of the Lord. I want to share some insights with you that the Lord shared with me. I want to start by sharing the story of the Ugly Duckling. The story shows that no matter where you are in your life span, there is the hope of experiencing a peaceful, joyful existence. Time is irrelevant because He's the creator of time. I learned that it doesn't matter how you started in life if you can only see your true reflection before the end.

he original fairytale of the Ugly Duckling is about a young duckling who experiences rejection and is treated cruelly because he's different than the rest of his family. He finally finds his tribe, is accepted and flourishes.

The Ugly Duckling

nce upon a time, there was a kind, loving family that lived on a farm in Iowa. The father, mother and two young children loved animals, fresh-picked vegetables and fruit. Their parents planted crops and farmed the land while the young children cared for and fed the animals. In the corral, there were cows, chickens, ducks, roosters and all kinds of beautiful animals. Early one morning as the mother duck was sitting on her eggs to keep them warm before they hatched, she felt a little thump from underneath her. She stood up to see what was happening and lo and behold, a small head popped through the shell of an egg. *Pop, pop, pop,* one by one, little heads popped out of their shells.

This happened five times, but wait, there was one egg left! It was the largest egg, and it didn't pop! All of the other little ducklings were looking around in wonder, excited to be in a brand-new place. Their loving mother looked on them proudly. They were so cute that she stood there for quite a while and admired them. She almost forgot that there was one more. She walked up to it and looked closer to see if there were any cracks in the shell. Her heart beat a little faster when she heard a strong pecking sound. *Peck, peck, peck,* and then a loud *pop*! A huge head appeared out of the shell. The mother watched in amazement as large feet, a large neck, white feathers, and dark legs appeared. She watched as it waddled over to the other baby ducklings.

Their eyes widened as they looked at their sibling, who appeared bigger, stronger and now appeared to be the big brother of the group. The mother and all of the little ducklings headed back toward the farmyard. All of the other animals were lazily moving around, enjoying the beautiful sunshine that was beaming upon the yard, when the mother duck and her newborn ducklings walked into the yard. There was a deafening silence. The cocks stop crowing, the cows stop mooing, and the birds stop singing. Everyone was focused entirely on the mother and her young ones. Finally, a loudmouth biddy spoke up and said, "what an ugly creature!" The mother was devastated, the siblings embarrassed, and the odd duckling was crushed in spirit.

His mother and siblings didn't speak up for him because they didn't know what to say. He felt as if he was no longer a part of the family or this community. He felt lonely and rejected. He wished he was invisible. The situation worsened as his siblings refused him, and his mother grew ashamed of him. The barnyard animals teased him mercilessly. The cows continually moo-ed him away. The hens mocked his looks, his movements, and his tears. He felt as if no one could ever really love him. He decided to go away without telling his family.

He chose a bad time to leave because he hadn't learned that seasons change and winter was coming. He wasn't prepared as he set out on his journey. The snow started falling softly and turned into a blizzard. The wind was blowing furiously and he was partially blinded by the snow. He was just about frozen and wanted to lie down when he spotted a barn. He peeped through the door and took in the scene. There was a variety of animals in the barn and they each had their own space. He timidly nudged the door open and asked if he could come in. They allowed him to come in but they weren't willing to share their straw, stalls and other small comforts. The animals made him sleep in a corner in the back of the barn.

He spent a long cold winter alone eating the scraps of the other animals. He observed the ease with which the animals related to each other. No one ever approached him. He remained isolated, lonely and sad. Finally, spring arrived and he continued on his journey. Approximately six miles down the road, he spotted a pond and saw the most amazingly beautiful birds. They had long graceful necks and beautiful white feathers. They were frolicking, twirling, diving and swimming. He longed to join them, but he was afraid. He was so fearful of rejection that he didn't go into the water. He was just plain scared. Finally, one of the beautiful creatures called to him to join them. He could hardly believe his ears! This was the first time that anyone had ever said a kind word to him. He timidly stepped into the water and immediately felt surrounded by beauty. He felt accepted and loved. He dove, played, and immersed himself in the wonders of those glorious waters. He was almost overwhelmed by his sense of newfound freedom. He had never experienced such an exhilarating time in his entire life.

A little girl and her mother came to the pond to watch the beautiful birds. The little girl's excitement showed in her voice as she exclaimed, "Look, mother, the new swan is the most beautiful of all!" The duckling was unaware of who she was referring to until the other swans gathered around him, admiring his beauty. He peered into the water and saw the most amazing thing! He saw himself as one of the most beautiful creatures on earth. He discovered that he wasn't a duck but had transformed into a beautiful swan!

He learned that he was a strong swimmer. The most amazing thing that he learned about himself was that he could fly! He rejoiced with his new family. When it was time for them to migrate, they invited him to go along with them and he accepted. He understood that he could no longer hold on to past experiences in the new life that had become available to him. He decided to forgive and forget all of the painful treatment and memories of the past. He rejoiced as he and the other swans flew to their next adventure.

The end

In this fairy tale, the little duckling experienced some horrific treatment at the hands of the barnyard animals. Rejection in any form is difficult to adjust to but when it comes from those who are close to you, it can be devastating. Although it looked as if he wouldn't survive, he rose to the challenge and overcame all odds. He fought through the pain and kept going in spite of the circumstances. The little duckling transformed into a strong beautiful swan with confidence and joy.

The True Tale of My Ugly Duckling Phase:

I was invited as a speaker at a Christian women's retreat in Myrtle Beach, South Carolina. As a minister of the gospel, I was excited about the theme of the retreat, which was "A Woman of Means." I knew that I was a woman of means and that I would use all of my resources to advance the kingdom. I was also excited about seeing all of the women of God and casually fellowshipping with them. I sat in the ballroom and began to look over some of the assigned topics such as "From Pain to Purpose," "From Light Affliction to Heavy Glory, "and "From Feather to Iron." My topic was "Iron Can Float." While browsing over the retreat topics, I glanced up and saw this beautiful young lady, and I smiled. The young lady smiled back, and I heard the words coming from my spirit, *"UGLY DUCKLING SYNDROME."* I immediately knew that it was God. I quickly turned my head away from her because I was afraid that He wanted me to give her a word of exhortation about what I heard. Every fiber of my being was resisting. I got up and went to my room alone to pray for her. I prayed that she would receive her healing and the revelation of who she is in Christ. Although I wondered what He wanted me to do with that word, I was afraid to ask.

While I contemplated what happened, the Lord answered my thoughts. He said, "Why don't you tell her how I delivered you from the Ugly Duckling Syndrome?" I was shocked, puzzled, confounded and speechless! I said Lord, "I have never considered myself ugly." He said, "This isn't about looks." He began to share with me how I previously operated within that syndrome. He flashed a vision of me from my childhood. I was out playing, and children were calling me names. They called me skinny with a witch nose, they called me other things, but those were the ones that stuck out. He asked me what I did when that happened, I said, "Nothing; I just went into the house and read books because I loved to read." He said, "You withdrew and isolated yourself. That is the way you processed your pain." Those three words came up again, *"UGLY DUCKLING SYNDROME."* Wow! By now my mind was racing! I wanted to know more, so I took out a pad and started writing about what He was revealing to me. I looked up the word *syndrome*, and learned it's "a predictable, characteristic pattern of behavior, action, etc. that tends to occur under certain circumstances." I realized that under certain conditions such as stress, uncertainty or insecurity, I would always retreat to a book. I spent long lonely years with not only my nose buried in a book but my heart, my soul and my mind. People, places, and their stories captivated me.

The Lord didn't let up. He fast-forwarded me to a vision of my teenage years. I was in the gym with a lot of girls, and we were preparing to try out for cheerleading. Some of the girls went up and did their cheers as the cheerleading coach took notes. A few of those girls were good at cheering, some were mediocre, but my turn was next. I was excited because I knew that I could do an excellent job of cheering, but the coach looked at me and said that I was too skinny and flat-chested! She didn't even let me try out! I was embarrassed, ashamed and most of all, I was devastated. I went home and never told anyone that I tried out to be a cheerleader. I buried the memory. I honestly didn't know the impact of that incident until the Lord revealed it to me.

When I looked back, I remembered that she was a skinny woman with a large chest. She wouldn't have made her own team if she went by her stated criteria. I don't know if she should've allowed me to try out and made up an excuse for why I didn't make it, or stated the physical qualifications beforehand. Maybe that was the way she processed her pain; I don't know. I just know that the incident caused me tremendous pain. The Lord said, "You withdrew from the children that hurt you and that was okay." He then explained to me that the kids had no authority over me. The cheerleading coach was a person in authority. She caused a breach in the spirit when she said that I couldn't try out.

God shared that the enemy used her to break every spiritual law associated with her position. She created an opening in the spirit that allowed the enemy to set up strongholds in my life. He said that she struck at the core of who God called me to be. He asked me, "what does a cheerleader do in the natural?" I replied, "cheerleaders encourage and motivate people to get into the game. They inspire the players to win and gain victory." He asked, "what does a Prophet do in the spiritual realm?" I said, "they encourage people in the Lord, they pray and inspire people to seek God and the Kingdom." He said, "you're a spiritual cheerleader. You would have been one of the best on that squad." By then I was weeping because the conversation was getting deep. He asked why it took so long to answer my call into the ministry, I said, "because I was shy." He said, *"UGLY DUCKLING SYNDROME."* He then began to share some of **the classic Characteristics of the Ugly Duckling Syndrome:**

- Never fitting in; feeling constantly out of place or unable to connect with people.
- Never feeling quite good enough; valuing others above yourself.
- Being a loner; preferring to be alone more than with people.
- May be a perfectionist; everything has to be perfect for you to feel good about it.
- Introvert; Being a shy reticent person; if you abhor revealing your thoughts or feelings to another.
- May be a workaholic; staying busy to fill a void in your life

- Not allowing others in your space; doesn't want to interact with others
- May be a people-pleaser; afraid of rejection
- May have a wandering spirit; always seeking acceptance
- May overcompensate; Continuous studies to become intellectual giants
- May be an underachiever; hesitant to take chances
- Perhaps an overachiever; trying to prove your worth
- May develop a fear of success and unknowingly sabotage their own success
- May develop a fear of failure because of low self-esteem
- May be very hard on themselves because of previous failures
- May feel like a victim because of past victimization
- May feel inadequate because of self-rejection
- Perhaps eccentric because of feeling different
- May be sad, depressed, dispirited
- May go from relationship to relationship looking for acceptance while asking in their hearts, do you see the worth or beauty in me?

So, I asked the Lord, when did I get delivered? He then took me to my message at the retreat which was, 'Iron Can Float." I preached from this passage of scripture:

2 Kings 6:1-7
¹And the sons of the prophets said unto Elisha, Behold now, the place where we dwell with thee is too strait for us. ² Let us go, we pray thee, unto Jordan, and take thence every man a beam, and let us make us a place there, where we may dwell. And he answered, Go ye.³And one said, Be content, I pray thee, and go with

thy servants. And he answered I will go. ⁴ So he went with them. And when they came to Jordan, they cut down wood. ⁵ But as one was felling a beam, the axe head fell into the water: and he cried, and said, Alas, master! for it was borrowed.⁶ And the man of God said, Where fell it? And he shewed him the place. And he cut down a stick, and cast it in thither, and the iron did swim.⁷ Therefore said he, Take it up to thee. And he put out his hand and took it.

I taught about the young prophets serving under their mentor Elisha. They decided their lives were too confining. They wanted to build their own ministries and dwelling place. During the building process, one of the young prophets dropped the iron ax head in the water. The ax head is symbolic of the word of God as a tool to build. They were devastated because it was borrowed. I ministered about Elisha working a miracle and making iron float by throwing a stick in the water. He used a stick to locate the iron. The water is symbolic of the Spirit. The Lord said, "over the years as you came to this retreat, every time Pastor Carolyn called you in for an assignment, she located you in the spirit, and threw a stick in the water! Every time she threw the stick you rose a little higher. Now you have floated to the top! What she did for you, go and do likewise. I worked a miracle in you, and now I want to work miracles through you!"

I never imagined that the ministry of the word was going deep down into the crevices of my heart. The word exposed deep-rooted hurt, unexpressed emotions and unfounded fears in my life. God took the sword of the Spirit and severed the unkind, careless words spoken over my life. He cut away the bewilderment, pain, and dejection. So, I say to the beautiful swans that may look like a duck, walk like a duck, and quack like a duck, it is time to rise to the top that you may see your reflection in the water. The scripture says that Christ loved the church and gave Himself for it; that He might sanctify and cleanse it with the washing of water by the word (Eph.5:25- 26). Rise up in the word and declare, *"I'm not even a duck so what am I doing in this barnyard? I will never settle for chicken feed when I can feast on the word of God and rise to my kingly status. I belong to royalty! I'm not a duck!"*

Change your view oh, beautiful swan. All I had to do was change my perspective. I could have been a model with skinny legs and a flat chest. I left with the impression that I wasn't good enough. How many of us have felt that way after an encounter with a person that didn't know your value? The little duckling's mother didn't see the value of her child. The father was nowhere in the picture. How many of us have longed to have a loving father who knows our worth? We may have to acknowledge that the Heavenly Father who created us may be the only one who really knows how valuable we are. He not only knows, but He's willing to share how valuable you are with you.

I believe the moral of this story is about identity and self- image. I didn't know that I was created in the image and likeness of my Creator. I wasn't aware of my true identity. I accepted the opinion of others as to who I was. But now that the truth has set me free, I feel compelled to set others free. Freedom comes when you change your perspective. The little duckling was afraid most of his life. He was paralyzed by fear and his self-worth was wrapped into what others thought of him. He needed the freedom to discover who he was. Once he made a decision, his season began to change. It was a tough, cold season for him but he was being transformed even in that period of time. We all experience winter seasons, but it is imperative that we don't die in the winter. Imagine when spring came and he found his tribe. Oh, what a time he had.

Sometimes we have to decide that we need a change. We may have to change locations, jobs or friends. Whatever the case may be, you must realize that wherever you go, your baggage goes with you. You have to change within. Your mindset must be in alignment with who you are to become. Jesus was the perfect example of rejection and abuse. He became the ugly duckling for us. Isaiah 52:14 says His appearance was so disfigured beyond that of any human being and His form marred beyond human likeness. He who knew no sin became sin for us. Sin is ugly, but Calvary changed everything. Jesus was spat upon, mocked and rejected, but He stayed on the cross until the work was finished. When He cried, "It is finished," that meant the end. He received His beautiful glorified body.

Our story is still being written. We can remain ugly ducklings, or we can accept what He did for us. We're sons created in the image of the Father. The little duckling discovered that he was different at birth. I believe we'll find our true beauty in the process of the new birth. The process of discovering who we are usually starts with family. We know our names, our siblings, our parents, and our communities. You'll usually relate to dysfunction as an adult if you start out with a dysfunctional family.

My heart goes out to of all of the young men, women, and children who have been stunted in life by the Ugly Duckling Syndrome. I meet many young men who have never known a loving hug of a father just because he loves them. Sometimes they become disappointed and angry. Think of the children who are different than their peers or perceive themselves as different. We should make a special effort to let them know how valuable and loved they are. It may take very little effort. Perhaps a smile, a hug or a kind word will break through the feeling of being disconnected. I know that many others feel alone in a world with millions of people. Rejection, loneliness, and abandonment will sometimes cause mental strongholds. These are strong mindsets that won't allow us to walk in freedom. The scriptures tell of people whose lives reflect some of the same things that we experience.

I searched the scriptures to find someone that could relate to the story of the ugly duckling, and I found Joseph. The difference between Joseph and I is the fact that he knew he had a father that loved him. His father covered him with love and gave him a coat of many colors. I can't read Jacob's mind, but if I gave my child a coat of many colors, each color would represent something. They would represent love, joy, peace, temperance and the other fruit of the spirit. Although Joseph was an ugly duckling to his brothers, his father pondered in his heart the peculiarities that made his youngest son different. He was shunned, mocked and rejected by his brothers, just like the little duckling. His brothers stripped him of his identity because without that coat; he was just like them. There was nothing to distinguish him. I feel that the garment of righteousness given by my Heavenly Father has separated me from being just like everyone else. Even as his brothers placed the blood on his clothing to signify his death, I feel that I have been covered with the blood of Jesus to signify my death to sin, sickness, and disease.

They threw Joseph into a pit of loneliness, despair, betrayal, and hurt but he was comforted by the fact that his father loved him. They sold him into slavery, but his bondage didn't appear to devastate him because he had a measure of freedom as an overseer of his master's house. Sometimes we settle for a measure of freedom because it feels okay until someone or something comes along to challenge that freedom. Potiphar's wife compromised that freedom, but he proved to be a man of integrity and chose to remain free. Joseph made the right decision when tested because he had a father that loved him. He was unjustly accused of being an ugly duckling. He knew that the ugliness wasn't within him, but he didn't verbalize it for fear of retaliation.

They threw him into a prison of accusation, torment, and hopelessness, but once again he rose to the top and everyone saw that the Lord was with him. Take note that Joseph was a young man and didn't have the experience that his father Jacob had with God. Joseph served his father's God because his father loved him and would never lead him astray concerning whom to worship. He developed a relationship with God, and one day it paid off. His purpose for being born into that family finally manifested when he was called to the palace to interpret a dream for the king. He was promoted in the kingdom, reconciled with his family, and paved the way for future generations to be saved.

Prayer

Father, I thank You that You're so loving and kind. I'm completely overjoyed to realize that You're with me during my darkest hours. You're the light of the world, and You're perfect in all Your ways. I pray that those who read this will conclude that You're a loving father even when we're oppressed in this world. Help us to see the purpose for which we were born. Help us to move from pain to purpose. I love you, Father.

Healing Prompt

If you find yourself displaying some of the characteristics of the Ugly Duckling Syndrome, assess your situation and determine if perhaps you have adjusted your lifestyle to accommodate the syndrome. I'm talking about an occasional activity. I'm talking about consistent ways and means of coping with the stressors of life. Ask yourself,

"How do I process my pain?" I would suggest you find scriptures that speak to who you are in Christ. Pray those scriptures over your life until you really believe them. Acknowledge any positive aspects of your character. Confess those over your life with an attitude of gratitude. Be confident that the Creator has started a good work in you and He'll be faithful to complete it.

CHAPTER TWO

Honor thy Father and Mother

Malachi 4:5-6

⁵ Behold, I will send you Elijah the prophet before the coming of the great and dreadful day of the LORD: ⁶ And he shall turn the hearts of the fathers to the children, and the heart of the children to their fathers, lest I come and smite the earth with a curse.

We discussed the story of The Ugly Duckling in the previous chapter. I shared with you that once upon a time, that was me. I knew that it wasn't the end of the story because the Spirit of the Lord said so. I was instructed by the Lord to invite my family to hear my story. I did and ministered this message at our church the Sunday after returning from the beach. My family was listening intently. I could see that some of them were visibly affected by it, but I knew that what was happening had a far-reaching spiritual effect. People were delivered from The Ugly Duckling Syndrome, and others were healed from past hurts and pain. They understood through the message that pain is a process within itself. I pressed on and released what God would allow me to release at that time. I was excited that I'd gotten through the story; I felt it was no longer mine but whoever identified with it. They could now process their pain in a Godly way. I was relieved that I'd gotten through it with a measure of success.

We had altar ministry at the end of the message. I spotted my older sister and went to hug her. When I hugged her, the Spirit said, "surrogate mother," and because I was so sensitive to the voice of the Spirit at that time, I automatically said, "my surrogate mother." I then began to dialog with God aloud and said to Him, "I always wanted her to be my mother." When I heard myself say those words aloud, I began to cry because buried memories were beginning to surface and I wanted to go home to process what He was saying. I didn't go home because I previously registered to go to another service. I went to the service and the presence of God was very strong. The speaker preached: "Rest well, Be at Peace."

Afterward, the host wanted to give out gifts. She said that there was a ticket taped under someone's seat, everyone looked under their seat and couldn't find the ticket. She said, "we might have to play musical chairs or something." I simply slid to the empty chair directly beside me because I was a little tired and didn't feel like moving much.

The host said to me, "you're sitting in the seat with the ticket." The Spirit immediately impressed upon me that sometimes all it takes is a small shift to receive your blessings. She handed me a gift bag and asked me to open it. I opened it, and it was a Barnes and Noble's Nook. It didn't dawn on me what it was. The young lady in front of me told me it was a reader. For those of you that need clarification, it is an electronic tablet on which you read books, watch movies and other things. I felt the overwhelming love of the Lord so strongly that I began to weep. It was as if He was saying it was all right to read when I'm in pain.

The host asked if I had anything to say. I said I loved the presence of the Lord and that I'd shared a message revealing how I loved to read. I thought God just wanted to bless me with a personal gift of love. I was obedient and shared my story. I thought the personal testimony was finished, so I could rest well and be at peace, but it wasn't to be. I honestly didn't understand the significance of the gift until the Spirit of the Lord awakened me that night with painful memories in my life concerning my parents. I wanted to escape in a book but I couldn't this time because I no longer read to escape the pain, I read for pleasure. He brought to my attention the scripture in Exodus 20:12: "Honour thy father and thy mother: that thy days may be long upon the land which the Lord thy God giveth thee."

First, He showed me a ministry session in which I ministered to someone about forgiving their mother. In that session, the Spirit spoke to me and said I had to release my father. My father left when I was less than two years old and never returned, leaving my mother to raise five daughters. I had no recollection or memory of him. We heard that he moved to New York, but had no contact with him for almost forty years. Because of personal struggles, he came back into our lives after all of those years.

My two older sisters remembered him and accepted him without any drama or fanfare. I asked them how they felt about him just walking back into our lives as if nothing had happened. They said that they had no ill feelings towards him. My middle sister walked up to him and slapped him. I asked her what she felt at that time and she stated that she was probably angry. The sister close in age to me immediately drew close to him and became his primary caretaker. They remained close until his death. I later found out that as a child, he would take her with him regularly as he visited our community. I never knew him so I had no reaction whatsoever, or so I thought.

We were adjusting in our own ways. I observed him from a distance and found him to be talkative and charming. He was opinionated and didn't mind sharing his thoughts. I asked the Lord to forgive me for any ill feelings that I may have had. I didn't think I held any grudges against him until the Lord showed me my scorn for him.

God showed me that I would become angry whenever my father mentioned anything about how we were raising our kids. I vividly remembered how I wanted to curse him out but I couldn't because I was a Spirit-filled Christian. I began receiving revelation about why I resented my father even though I never knew him.

We're created in the image of a loving Father and our hearts will always long for a caring protector and provider. Before we're regenerated through the new birth, we project our thoughts, feelings, and emotions on an earthly father. We usually thrive when we have an earthly father who is loving and protective of us. When that person is missing, we almost always feel a void in our lives. Our mothers nurture, comfort and meet our basic needs of food clothing and guidance, but we still need that fatherly connection. If our fathers are detached, cruel, abusive or any other negative characteristic, we're sometimes influenced by that in our relationships with others, including God. We may think He isn't concerned about our welfare. We may unconsciously believe that He's just like our biological fathers. When we accept Jesus Christ as our Lord and Savior and God as our Father, we have to discern how we view Him. We should view Him as a loving, merciful, protective Father who has provided everything we need pertaining to life and godliness.

Later my father had a stroke, and I went to visit him a few times in the nursing home. He was upset because I didn't visit more often. He asked me how many times I'd been to see him since he'd been there. I smiled, ignored him and held my tongue, but when I got in the car to leave, I told my husband that I should have told him that I visited him more times than he'd ever visited me in my lifetime. I remember expressing the fact that his brother was more of a father to us than he ever was. I resented him, I rejected him, but in the end, I forgave him because my Heavenly Father said to release him.

Un-forgiveness holds us hostage to the pain of hurtful memories and sad thoughts. You go through your mind trying to reconstruct the story or possibly find a better ending, but sometimes you have to release the pain by forgiving. Honor and forgiveness aren't suggestions. They're commands. I would like to share some things about my mother with you. She was a pretty strong-willed woman. She raised five daughters. I don't ever recall being hungry or homeless. She suffered many illnesses, but she always recovered. I think she fought to live for her daughters. I know she was physically there for us, but I felt as if all of her emotional energy was spent trying to please an abusive boyfriend. I transferred my affection to my older sister who had kids of her own. I love my sister tremendously and I'm very grateful for the crucial part she has played in my life.

I believe my mother processed her pain through alcohol. I have always been grateful that she chose to do her best to raise us. I always thought that she could've done better in her own life, but I didn't know that she was processing her pain. If she were here to tell her story of The Ugly Duckling Syndrome, I believe her story would have been closer to the original story. The story was modified for children. In the original story, the mother hen resented being left by the father to raise her chicks. The original author of The Ugly Duckling said that parts of the story were too painful to tell, so it had to be edited. I've chosen to modify this portion of my story because the purpose of mentioning those painful memories isn't to reveal them but to heal them. I wouldn't bring honor to my parents by telling their story without giving them a chance to edit the parts they didn't want to be revealed.

My mother and one of my other sisters transitioned from this earth within the same week. I mourned them briefly, but God had prepared me by giving me an overwhelming desire to dance before their death. After the funeral, He spoke in that still small voice and said, "I turned your mourning into dancing. I have called you to do a work, and you can't have a long mourning period." I must say that I loved my mother, but I didn't always honor her. Now I not only love my parents but I honor them. It isn't because of anything they have done but for whom they are. I'm free in this chapter of my life. I feel no more shame, guilt, or pain. I'm moving from pain to purpose. I believe my purpose for being born into my family is found in the Biblical story of Joseph who was the youngest of Jacob's sons. God sent Joseph to Egypt ahead of his family to preserve future generations in the earth.

Future generations could be your children, great-great-grandchildren, or any others who are born after you. I believe I have been sent into the Kingdom to ensure that generations will come to the Lord and become Kingdom citizens. The story is found in Genesis 45:7 "and God sent me before you to preserve you a posterity in the earth, and to save your lives by a great deliverance."

I searched the scriptures again to find someone who could relate to the part of my story of honor and dishonor. I found that there are numerous dysfunctional families in the Bible and that I'm not the only one who somehow dishonored their parents. I saw Noah's son Ham and David's son Absalom.

> **Noah** (Genesis 6:7-8)
> *[7] And the LORD said, I will destroy man whom I have created from the face of the earth; both man, and beast, and the creeping thing, and the fowls of the air; for it repenteth me that I have made them.[8] But Noah found grace in the eyes of the LORD.*

The Bible proclaims that Noah found grace in the eyes of the Lord, which means he found favor with God. This grace allowed him to save his family when God was destroying all of humanity. So how does the story end?

Noah blessed his other two sons because of their respect and honor toward him. They covered his nakedness and refused to look at his weaknesses, his faults, or his drunkenness. They could have confronted the situation, but they chose to deliberately walk in an unusual way to cover his sins. I believe they loved their father because love covers a multitude of sins. The most important thing is that they honored their father. It wasn't the case with the youngest son. He saw his father naked and left him in that drunken state to run and tell his brothers. He didn't care that someone else could have seen his father naked. He didn't feel obligated to cover his father's sin. The consequences of his actions prove to be detrimental to future generations. Noah awakened, blessed Shem and Japheth, and pronounced a curse on Canaan, the descendants of Ham (Genesis 9:18-25).

I also studied the story of Absalom, David's son. The Bible declares that David's son Absalom was beautiful from head to toe (see 2 Samuel 14:25) but because of his dishonor towards his father, his story didn't end well.

His story became ugly when he killed his brother and tried to take over his father's kingdom. His father's former counselor advised him to openly shame his father by sleeping with his father's wives (2 Samuel 16:20-23).

There was no turning back for the young man then; he had to see his way through to the end. He took the advice of the counselor and used the same roof on which his father committed adultery with Bathsheba. By lying with his father's wives, he was in fact saying, this kingdom and all of its subjects belong to me now. Sometimes we inherit the good, the bad and the ugly from previous generations. Dishonor didn't bring him the glory that he thought it would. It was a sad ending because even after all of his destructive behavior, his father still loved him and wanted reconcile with him. He crossed the line by a wide margin. First, because he dishonored his father and second because he touched God's anointed King. He died tragically (2 Samuel 18:9-15).

Death was a high price to pay for dishonoring his father, but that is how the story ends. A word of caution here: once upon a time, David was a murderer and an adulterer. Although Absalom despised his father, he became the same thing. Don't become what you hate.

Prayer

Father, I thank you for the Blood of Jesus that can break every generational curse. I know that He became a curse for us and now sits at Your right-hand interceding for us. I pray and ask Your forgiveness for not abiding in Your word and honoring our parents. Create in us a clean heart and renew a right spirit within us. Thank You for placing Your commandments in our hearts. We know that

You commanded us to honor our mother and father and that's what we'll do. We receive the promise of a long life that is attached to the commandment. Amen

Healing Prompt

Few people can wound us as deeply as our family because we rarely allow anyone to get that close to us. There is a bond created through family ties that continues even through extreme pain. We have to purpose in our hearts that we'll allow the healing grace of God to saturate our hearts in the midst of offense. I won't pretend it'll be easy but it is necessary.

CHAPTER THREE

Trusting God

Psalm 127: 3

*Lo, children are an heritage of the LORD: and
the fruit of the womb is his reward.*

I was sound asleep after writing some of my stories concerning my mother and father. I woke up with memories of agonizing moments that I experienced with my children. The moment those memories surfaced, I felt fear, anxiety, worry, and intense pain. I don't think I know of any mother that hasn't felt some negative emotions about raising children in a society that sometimes appears hostile towards their offspring. Fear quickly bubbled to the surface. I was extremely disappointed and hurt that God wanted to access those painful moments that seemed to go on forever, but they were magnified by my desire for them to be over.

I began to wonder if I should stop telling my story because it felt like God didn't love me, if He did, He wouldn't hurt me like this. I withdrew from the presence of the Lord, nursing my pain. I felt I could no longer trust Him. I felt betrayed, wounded, dismayed, sad and lonely. I felt like sleeping. I didn't feel like reading. I never wanted to read again. I wanted my adult children safely back at home with me so I could have peace. I decided that I would never openly say anything about them without their permission. I wanted to stop the entire process because it was getting too intense. I went back to bed and was in a sound sleep when I heard the sound of the bathroom door closing. It was my husband coming back to bed. I asked him where he had been, he said to the bathroom. He asked if I heard him get up and I said no. The Spirit said, "I placed you in a deep sleep so that I may extract some memories."

I was lying on my back, and I felt as if I had wings and some birds were trying to get under my wings. I quickly turned on my side and closed both arms tight to myself. I laid in that position while the Spirit ministered to me about my protective feelings towards my children. He said, "The same way you feel about your children is the way I think of you. I would never hurt you. I'm protective of you. I hide you under my wings. You have other spiritual children that need to be nurtured, but if you don't allow them to get close enough to cause you pain, they'll never mature into beautiful swans. I love you and even though you don't trust me with your children, I trusted you with them." I was speechless as I realize that they're His and not mine! I'm merely a steward of everything that God has given me. I searched the scripture for Godly parents that had to place their children at the mercy and faithfulness of God, and I found an example in the story of Zelophehad's daughters (Numbers 26:33).

> *Numbers 27:4-7*
> *⁴ Why should the name of our father be done away from among his family, because he hath no son? Give unto us, therefore, a possession among the brethren of our father. ⁵ And Moses brought their cause before the Lord. ⁶ And the Lord spake unto Moses, saying, ⁷ The daughters of Zelophehad speak right: thou shalt surely give them possession of an inheritance among their father's brethren, and thou shalt cause the inheritance of their father to pass unto them.*

These five daughters descended from a God-fearing man. He died, and because of the laws given by God to Moses, they couldn't inherit any land from their father. They were at the mercy of the males in their families. They were distraught but determined to petition Moses to rectify the injustice. They asked Moses, "Why should our father's name be done away with just because he had no sons. He served God, and his name should be remembered." Moses took their petition to God, and He says, "they're right, change the laws so that not only will they benefit, but other females as well."

Whew! That was powerful to me because Zelophehad means "without fear!" A fearless man raised those girls and instilled that quality in them. They weren't afraid to approach Moses and ask for what they felt rightfully belonged to them. They were pioneers who knew the law was unjust and weren't afraid to challenge it. They were instrumental in speaking up for an entire nation. They were fearless! Their father was a righteous man and they used that fact to make a case before Moses. Perhaps when we're fearful, we should present our case to the Lord. The Bible says perfect love casts out fear. I choose to have my love perfected so that I may live a fearless lifestyle.

Prayer

Father, I make a conscious decision to trust You in every area of my life. I realize that the Earth is the Lord's and the fullness thereof, so I choose to live a fully committed life dedicated to the service and work of the Lord. Be glorified in my life and allow me to see my seed blessed and favored by You.

Healing Prompt

Begin to make a conscious decision to trust in the providence of God concerning your loved ones. Try to keep in mind that He cares. Dedicate your children, your marriage and other family members to the Lord. Ask for peace.

CHAPTER FOUR

Sleeping Beauty Syndrome

Ephesians 5:14

*Wherefore he saith, Awake thou that sleepest, and arise
from the dead, and Christ shall give thee light.*

The sound of a loud alarm clock roused me. I knew from previous experience that it wasn't a natural alarm but a spiritual sound to get my attention. I got up and went into the living room. I was so sleepy I could hardly keep my eyes open. I got on my knees, but the sleep was overwhelming. I listened for that still small voice, but it didn't come. I was fighting to stay awake because I felt God's presence, but He wasn't saying anything. I arose and sat on the sofa, still trying to wake up. I then got the impression that this shift to another position had released something in the spirit. Revelation began to flow concerning the body of Christ being asleep in God's presence. Proverbs 6:9-11 came to me: "⁹ How long wilt thou sleep, O sluggard? When wilt thou arise out of thy sleep? ¹⁰ Yet a little sleep, a little slumber, a little folding of the hands to sleep:¹¹ So shall thy poverty come as one that travelleth, and thy want as an armed man."

It is a fact that some Christians have fallen into a slumbering pattern just like the fairytale *Sleeping Beauty*.

ORIGINAL VERSION

In the original fairytale, a mean-spirited fairy curses a beautiful princess with death. A good fairy changes the curse to allow her to sleep for years until a prince discovers her and falls in love. He awakens her with a kiss. They marry and live happily ever after.

MY VERSION

Sleeping Beauty

Once upon a time, there was a lovely couple who happened to be the king and queen of a small nation called the Netherlands. They were remarkably excited to welcome their firstborn child into the world. She was a beautiful princess.

They announced her arrival throughout the kingdom and prepared to introduce her to the elite population in the domain. They sent invitations to the top officials in the land and then invited others to the ceremony. They knew that there was a particular class of people in the kingdom called Fairies, who would bring gifts and release best wishes upon the child.

They invited all of those that were in the Royal Book of Fairies. They didn't know that one of them was previously banished from the kingdom many years ago for unkind deeds. She received an invitation and came along with the others. When the time came to release best wishes over the child, all of the other fairies released their best. The banished fairy looked at the child and remembered the royal decree that expelled her from the kingdom. She issued a curse over the child: "when you're a teenager, you'll have a terrible accident that'll cause you to die." All of the courts gasped in horror. The guards rushed to the mean, witchy fairy and ushered her out of the castle. The other fairies gathered around the poor child and discussed how the curse could be broken. They realized that they couldn't overrule the senior fairy's curse, but they could alter it by using their powers as one. They decided to proclaim that the accident wouldn't claim her life, but she would fall into a deep sleep for a hundred years. They also declared that a young prince with a pure heart would come along and fall in love with her and wake her up. They all agreed and began to release those words over her.

The princess grew up, and one day while running through the castle having fun, she fell down a long flight of stairs. The doctors arrived and found her unconscious. They were unable to wake her up. She remained in that state for years. She never aged; it was as if she was suspended in time. The castle was turned into a museum, but she remained in a small room beside the steps of the attic.

One day a traveler from another kingdom heard of her plight and decided that he wanted to see if the rumors were true. He was the Prince of Wales. He entered the castle with the other visitors but sneaked away to look into the rooms that were off-limits to the public. He spotted a tiny door beside the steps to the attic and went inside. Once inside, he was astonished to see the most beautiful young lady in the kingdom, lying there in a peaceful sleep. He stared for hours until he heard over the intercom that the museum was closing. He touched her hand slightly and gently kissed her beautiful cheek. Her eyes opened. He was astounded! He explained to her why he was there, expressing his adoration and love for her. He asked her to marry him. She smiled and accepted his proposal. They were married and lived happily ever after.

The End

One view of this story is that of the mean-spirited fairy who released a curse over the young princess. The other aspect is that of the innocent child who had no input in the direction that her life would take because of the evil fairy. She cast a spell, which influenced other fairies to intervene, and then the drama began.

Many times, the spiritual climate within the body of Christ becomes toxic because of jealousy, backbiting, strife, and arguments. When these things happen, people tend to withdraw from fellowship with others and establish a sleeping pattern. God showed me that some members of the body would come to spiritual poverty because their desire to sleep is stronger than their desire for fellowship with Him. They're dull of hearing. They'll become void of understanding about spiritual matters. I'm not referring to natural sleep; I'm referring to spiritual sleep. It happens when you become unconscious towards the things of God. Some Christians will become spiritually bankrupt. They'll fold their hands and slumber when life becomes too painful. The pain won't go away just because you choose to sleep.

The word will deliver you from every pain imaginable if you allow it to penetrate your heart. The word of God is quick, sharp, and powerful and if used correctly will divide the truth from a lie and cut to the root of the pain.

I was fascinated by this story because it appears that love was all it took for the beautiful princess to wake up. The criterion was "if a prince with a pure heart were to fall in love with her, that would wake her up." That is powerful to me because I know that God so loved the world that He gave his only begotten Son, that whosoever believeth in Him should not perish but have everlasting life. My God, love kept Jesus up on that cross! Love caused Him to be rejected, whipped, and forsaken. There is no greater love than a man would lay down his life for his friends. Passion should propel every Christian to tell about the greatest love of all.

I believe the church has fallen asleep in some cases. I see her as a sleeping giant. Believers have the power within them to cause an explosion wherever they find themselves. The marketplace, educational institutions, and such places are all in dire need of the body of Christ to wake up and become a reckoning force in this world. We're leaders because our King is a leader and we have been endowed with His power. Love doesn't want humanity to experience destruction. Love isn't hateful, evil or pretentious; it is pure. It seems the Bride of Christ is in a holding pattern. We have put our lives on hold until the perfect circumstances present themselves. Sleeping beauty is also in a waiting pattern: waiting for the right time; waiting for the right cause; waiting for the right place; waiting for Mr. Right; waiting for prosperity; waiting, waiting, waiting.

Sleeping beauty, if you're waiting for Mr. Right to come along and wake you up, I declare that Mr. Right has already arrived. He came, He bled and died, but He rose with all power in His hands. He slept for three days, and for us who needed salvation, that was the longest three days in history. So, if you want Him to wake you up, I say unto you, it's done. God declares "but now is Christ risen from the dead, and become the first fruits. Of them, that slept. (1 Cor. 15:20)" Because He got up, we can get up. My present philosophy is live until you die and then live again.

Possible Characteristics of the Sleeping Beauty Syndrome include:

- Sleepwalking through life
- Always looking for something exciting to keep you awake
- Will start projects and never complete them
- Pays more attention to the flesh than the spirit
- May avoid confrontation, go along to get along
- May go from job to job and never settle in a career
- May get stuck in a time warp
- May find it difficult to make decisions

If you identify with these characteristics, you may need to acquaint yourself with the voice of the Lord.

> **Hebrews 12:26-28**
> *26 Whose voice then shook the earth: but now he hath promised, saying, Yet once more I shake not the earth only, but also heaven. 27 And this word, Yet once more, signifieth the removing of those things that are shaken, as of things that are made, that those things which cannot be shaken may remain. 28 Wherefore we receiving a kingdom which cannot be moved, let us have grace, whereby we may serve God acceptably with reverence and godly fear:*

His kingdom has come on Earth because His kingdom is within us. The gospel is a powerful earth-shaking force that'll cause nations to wake up and acknowledge the Prince of Peace. So, if we're waiting for a prince, He has already come. If you're waiting for a king, He's the King of Kings and Lord of Lords. If you're waiting for the curse to be broken, guess what? It has already been broken (Galatians 3:13).

Wake up and stop making excuses as to why you aren't living life in the fullest sense. Tell your excuses to take a nap for a hundred years while you live an abundant life. We tend to look at others and decide to wait before acting on my dreams, my passion or my desires. That's the wrong attitude. Wake up and smell the roses while you can. I found a version of sleeping beauty in Matthews 25:1-10

> *¹ Then shall the kingdom of heaven be likened unto ten virgins, which took their lamps, and went forth to meet the bridegroom. ² And five of them were wise, and five were foolish. ³ They that were foolish took their lamps, and took no oil with them: ⁴ But the wise took oil in their vessels with their lamps. ⁵ While the bridegroom tarried, they all slumbered and slept. ⁶ And at midnight there was a cry made, Behold, the bridegroom cometh; go ye out to meet him. ⁷ Then all those virgins arose and trimmed their lamps. ⁸ And the foolish said unto the wise, Give us of your oil; for our lamps are gone out.⁹ But the wise answered, saying, Not so; lest there be not enough for us and you: but go ye rather to them that sell, and buy for yourselves.¹⁰ And while they went to buy, the bridegroom came; and they that were ready went in with him to the marriage: and the door was shut.*

I was intrigued they all slumbered and slept. I would have been unable to sleep in anticipating the Bridegroom's arrival. I won't pretend that I know *why* they slept, but I want to look at *how* they slept. Some slept peacefully because they were prepared for His coming. They weren't only beautiful but also wise. The others weren't prepared. I don't care how beautiful you are if you choose to be careless or foolish with your life and time on this earth, you'll regret it. So, I say to all the sleeping beauties, it is time to wake up. It is time to take your rightful place in the kingdom. It is time to realize that the Bridegroom, Prince, King, or however you choose to label Him, is coming for you because He loves you. That's a promise.

Prayer

Father, I choose to be alert and attentive to Your voice. I won't sleepwalk through life because Jesus came that I might have life more abundantly. The price has already been paid for my salvation, and therefore I know my value. Be glorified in my life as You waken my ear morning-by-morning to hear Your words.

Healing Prompt

As you become more alert in the spirit, become active in servitude by giving your time, talents and gifts to advance the kingdom. Become a doer of the word and not a hearer only.

CHAPTER FIVE

The Emperor's New Clothes

Colossians 3:12

Put on, therefore, as the elect of God, holy and beloved, bowels of mercies, kindness, humbleness of mind, meekness, longsuffering;

he original story is about an emperor who loves attention and is fascinated with clothes. He loves the attention he gets by donning the finest outfits. He's duped into wearing an invisible suit and most of his subjects go along with the charade. A young lad finally exposes the charade with the statement "The Emperor has no clothes on".

The Emperor's New Clothes

nce upon a time, there was an Emperor who loved the limelight. He loved fancy cars, fine dining, and extravagant parties. Everything he did was on a grand scale. He was obsessed with appearances and how others perceived him. He especially loved clothes and sought out all of the most prominent fashion designers in the world. They dropped whatever they were designing for others to answer his call. They rushed to his side to inquire about his needs. He thought he needed to be the first to wear any fashion because he always thought of himself as a trendsetter. He commissioned them to find the most excellent and most expensive material in all the world. They traveled extensively to accomplish their task. He appeared to be well pleased with their efforts and rewarded them generously. This went on for many years, as the designers always kept him informed of the latest fashion.

One year, a new fashion designer arrived on the scene. He was immediately recognized as the top designer throughout the kingdom. He designed for other Emperors as well as their wives. He discovered his passion for fashion while observing his mother who was a poor but efficient seamstress who earned decent wages. This designer didn't limit himself to designing for the rich and famous but used his skills to help the poor. He worked incognito to develop work uniforms for farm laborers. He designed weather-resistant clothing for those exposed to harsh climates. He designed protective wear for those exposed to environmental hazards. He did all of this secretly while creating for the rich and famous simultaneously.

One day the Emperor heard about a renowned designer and summoned him to his court. He arrived and inquired why he was there. The Emperor told him that it was getting too tedious to have so many fashion designers at his beck and call. He said that he would like for him to be his personal designer with the freedom to pick and choose what he wanted him to wear at all times. The Designer asked for a week to think about it, and the Emperor agreed.

The Designer thought long and hard. He hated to give up his custom of designing for the less fortunate. He continued thinking. Finally, he devised a plan. He thought to himself, I can keep my work with the poor and have the Emperor finance it. He went to the Emperor and asked for a contract to travel to every nation in the world to look for exotic materials. He also requested the freedom to buy designs from other designers in remote places. The Emperor was so thrilled to think that he would be the most fashionable person in the entire world that he agreed. The Designer went across the globe employing poor people of other nations to sew his designs for the emperor. He bought and used their materials, which weren't the most exceptional quality but suitable for a few uses.

The Emperor never suspected anything because he rarely wore the same outfit twice and never left his kingdom. He continued his practice of having extravagant parties to show off his new clothes. Everyone in his court was actually weary of the charade, but they held their peace because they didn't want to offend the Emperor. They knew that no matter how many parties, clothes and acquaintances that he surrounded himself with, it would all be in vain.

One day, new servants came to work in the palace. It was a foreign couple from a very remote location such as the Amazon Jungle. They didn't understand English very well, but they had a young son who was learning English. One evening as the court was crowded with people for a grand ball, the Emperor wanted to make his grand entrance to show off his new clothes. As he entered, there was a chorus of oohs and aahs. The people were saying things such as magnificent, fabulous and excellent! The new servants pushed through the crowd to serve the Emperor. They had their son with them to interpret if needed. When they got to the royal seat where the emperor was seated, the little boy cried out, look, "Mother and Father! The Emperor and I have the same clothes!" The buzz that went throughout the kingdom can still be heard to this day.

The End

In this tale of the Emperor's New Clothes, it isn't the clothes that dominate the story, but the Emperor's struggle with pride, people and position. I chose to tell this story through the eyes of the church of Jesus Christ based upon Revelation 1:5-6

> *⁵ And from Jesus Christ, who is the faithful witness, and the first begotten of the dead, and the prince of the kings of the earth. Unto him, that loved us, and washed us from our sins in his own blood, ⁶ And hath made us kings and priests unto God and his Father; to him be glory and dominion forever and ever. Amen.*

For so long we have portrayed ourselves as a Kingdom of priests that adheres to the standard of righteousness that God requires. In the narrative of this story, people are looking at us because we're kings. The problem is that we cover up our insecurities, pain and other emotions with an invisible suit. Humor, anger, deception or whatever else may be your suit, but you can see right through it. We look good, smell good and pretend that everything is okay. What we actually should do is make an appointment with the master tailor and get fitted with the best quality material. We have gotten caught up in appearances to our detriment.

We overlook spiritual lawlessness because of our positions and substitute the anointing with a title. Sometimes we accept and perpetuate a designer gospel. Someone comes along like the designer in the fairy tale and convinces us that it isn't politically correct to adhere to Biblical standards. They tell us that the Bible is obsolete, so our local churches become social clubs with occasional motivational speeches that warm our hearts. We make promises, saying God wants us to have the best of everything, the best houses, cars, and cash. We neglect to tell the world that God has already given us His best when he gave us His son. We mimic the people in the fairy tale. We pretend we see the power of the gospel when all we really see is good entertainment. We look at each other and compare ourselves. We compete to see who looks the best as we prance in front of the world like the Emperor.

Possible Characteristics of the Emperor Syndrome:

- Obsessed with appearances
- Loves attention
- Prideful
- Has feelings of inadequacy
- May pretend or play-act
- May have a strong need to be loved and accepted

God admonishes us to put on the whole armor of God that we may be able to stand against the wiles of the devil. He has strategically set up inroads into the church and weakened our testimony. The word of our testimony is about the power of the risen Savior to deliver us from destruction. We're influential people and can only be overtaken by our confession and permission. It is imperative that we're dressed appropriately. The helmet of salvation is pretty useless without the shield of faith. There is no excuse for allowing the world to see us in an undressed state, pretending they can see our garments of righteousness.

The Emperor's subjects kept the pretense among themselves. His leaders never challenged his obsessive behavior. Perhaps they were fearful of being dismissed. They may have even been anticipating a promotion. But in the real world, promotion comes from God. We can look at King Nebuchadnezzar in Daniel 4:30-31:

> *30 The king spake, and said, Is not this great Babylon, that I have built for the house of the kingdom by the might of my power, and for the honour of my majesty? 31 While the word was in the king's mouth, there fell a voice from heaven, saying, O king Nebuchadnezzar, to thee, it is spoken; The kingdom is departed from thee.*

Nebuchadnezzar became lifted up in pride because of his great exploits in conquering all of the nations around him. God warned him in a dream that if he didn't acknowledge the true God of Heaven as the one who enabled him to rule other nations, judgment would come to him. Nebuchadnezzar refused to accept the counsel of Daniel who gave the interpretation of the dream. He was walking in the palace admiring his accomplishments when judgment came. He lost his mind and remains in that state for seven years as prophesied.

It took a lot to get King Nebuchadnezzar to the place of humility when all he had to do was listen to the prophet whose counsel was sound. The fact is, Nebuchadnezzar accomplished some great things, but the truth is that it was done by the mighty hand of God. He acknowledged this at the end of seven long years (Daniel 4:30-31,37). Humility is the path to exaltation (1 Peter 5:6).

The Emperor never acknowledged his deception in our fairytale. Those around him went along with the diabolical plot to make him look good. Their lack of candor was a great disservice to him. He didn't have accountability partners within the whole kingdom. He strutted, pranced, and pretended and no one cared enough about him to pull his prideful coattail...shame, shame, shame, but wait, there was someone. A child uncontaminated by the popular opinion of others, blurted out the truth ('The Emperor is wearing my clothes"). Although the child spoke the truth, the Emperor didn't acknowledge his statement because that would have been too embarrassing. The lad was the least likely to affect change because he didn't have any prominent standing within the kingdom. He was but a small child and of little stature (perhaps like the man in this true story):

> **Zacchaeus** (Luke 19:2-4)
> *² And, behold, there was a man named Zacchaeus, which was the chief among the publicans, and he was rich. ³ And he sought to see Jesus who he was; and could not for the press, because he was little of stature. ⁴ And he ran before and climbed up into a sycamore tree to see him: for he was to pass that way.*

I don't know what caused Zacchaeus to go to such extreme measures to get a glimpse of Jesus. Perhaps he heard of miracles, healings, and deliverances that had taken place as he traveled from town to town. Maybe he heard of disciples that left everything they had to follow Jesus. Perhaps he wanted to know if this was the new Emperor. He may have wanted to see if this Emperor was appropriately dressed. I know it's rare to see rich men climbing trees just to get a glance at other men. Zacchaeus was on a mission to see who Jesus was. It wouldn't have been enough for the disciples to say that He was clothed with power from on high. It wouldn't have been enough for the Pharisees and Sadducees to tell him that Jesus was the King of the Jews. He had to see for himself. He laid down his pride, status, and position and went into the crowd. He was pressed in on every side and couldn't see above the shoulders of taller men. No one offered to let him go to the front of the crowd because they were curious too. Perhaps this Jesus had some special powers or unusual words to lift the oppression imposed by the Romans. Zacchaeus didn't waste time trying to bribe someone to open up the way for him to get to the front. He looked around and spotted a tree. He climbed with determination, got to the top and waited. Luke 19:5-10 explains what happened next:

> ⁵ And when Jesus came to the place, he looked up, and saw him, and said unto him, Zacchaeus, make haste, and come down; for today I must abide at thy house. ⁶ And he made haste, and came down, and received him joyfully. ⁷ And when they saw it, they all murmured, saying, that he was gone to be guest with a man that is a sinner. ⁸ And Zacchaeus stood, and said unto the Lord: Behold, Lord, the half of my goods I give to the poor; and if I have taken anything from any man by

false accusation, I restore him fourfold. ⁹ And Jesus said unto him, This day is salvation come to this house, forasmuch as he is also a son of Abraham. ¹⁰ For the Son of man is come to seek and to save that which was lost.

He called him down from his lofty position and went home with him as the crowd murmured and complained about him being a guest of a sinner. Zacchaeus was overjoyed and didn't take the time to answer his critics because Jesus was in the house. I believe Zacchaeus saw the invisible suit through the eyes of faith. He was the perfect host, all the while examining his guest closely. He heard through the grapevine that Jesus was a glutton and winebibber, so he gave Him the finest food and wine in the house. He watched for His response. The food or the wine didn't move Jesus because He had a far higher purpose for being there. Zacchaeus was a prominent figure in the kingdom of darkness with a lot of influence. He needed what Jesus had more than Jesus needed what he had, so, they communed and fellowshipped with one another.

He saw that Jesus was clothed adequately with humility and love for mankind. His feet were shod with the preparation of the gospel of peace. Conviction began to stir in the heart of Zacchaeus. He longed to right every wrong that he had ever done. He wanted to give to the poor. He wanted to restore the lives of his previous clients. Jesus said the very words that Zacchaeus wanted to hear, "This day salvation comes to this house." He realized that Jesus called him down to lift him up to spiritual heights that he never dreamed of. I believe that if we would get out of the parade business and get to the business of the Kingdom, many souls would hear those same words spoken by Jesus over 2,000 years ago. Someone needs to know that we're clothed with the garment of righteousness and have the authority to present the garment of salvation to them.

There are multitudes in the valley of decision that are waiting and watching to see if we have the answers to their problems. We're somebody's solution. Jesus says he came to seek and to save that which was lost. We're ministers of reconciliation, so that should be our mission too. I believe that sometimes we may have to take drastic measures to attain spiritual heights for salvation to come to our homes, as well as our friends and loved ones' homes. Climb a tree, tear a hole in a roof, press through a crowd, yell loudly, get out of the boat and walk on water. We should do whatever it takes to fulfill the great commission.

Zacchaeus' status was elevated on that day. When God anointed David in the midst of his brethren, he didn't become king the same day. He continued to lead sheep before becoming a leader of men. He fought lions and bears before becoming a warrior in the army. He subdued giants before becoming a giant himself. You may have the title of king, but you have to become the king that God desires you to be. I think we need the proper attire so others can see the garments of righteousness on us. So, I declare to you today: Emperor, your tailor, is waiting for you. Make sure you're dressed properly (Ephesians 6:10-17; 1 Peter 2:9).

Prayer

Father, I thank You for bringing this word of exhortation to our attention. I pray that we won't walk in deception or pride. Help us not to be seduced by the cares of this world. Remind us that we have been translated out of darkness into the marvelous light. I pray that our light would shine brightly and dispel the darkness. We glorify You, Father.

Healing prompt

Identify any areas in your life that the Holy Spirit is ministering to you. Submit your will to the Lord and refuse to be lifted up in pride. Practice humility and allow God to elevate you. Examine yourselves to see if there is anything that has you hiding in fear, shame or distress. Ask the Lord to heal and deliver, that you may be totally free.

CHAPTER SIX

Rapunzel Syndrome

Romans 12:1

*I beseech you, therefore, brethren, by the mercies of
God, that ye present your bodies a living sacrifice, holy,
acceptable unto God, which is your reasonable service.*

n the original story, Rapunzel is locked in a tower by a possessive adoptive mother. The only access to her is by her exceptionally long beautiful hair. She has a wonderfully melodic voice and consoles herself by composing and singing romantic love songs. Eventually, a suitor nearing the castle hears her and risks his life climbing her hair to win her heart.

MY VERSION

Rapunzel

nce upon a time, there was a pretty, carefree young lady named Rapunzel, who loved singing, dancing and taking adventurous trips with the youth group at her small community church. She lived in a quiet town with her parents, where most of the neighbors knew each other. She would go next door to do homework with her friend Brittney. Brittney's parents always welcomed Rapunzel into their home and provided snacks for the two girls. One day Rapunzel's father came home and said that his plant was closing and he had to find a new job. The plant shut down, and months later he was still looking for a job. He finally landed a job in a much larger city about two hundred miles away. They didn't want to go but felt they didn't have a choice. They moved to the town which was immensely different from what they were used to. There was lots of traffic, loud noises, sirens blasting and many other things that concerned them. They missed their small quiet neighborhood. They moved into an apartment on the top floor of a ten-story building. They always heard children crying and adults yelling late into the evening. They knew that they should try to make the best of their situation, so they settled in. Rapunzel's mother enrolled her in school and found herself a job. She stayed in the apartment alone after school until her parents came home in the evening. She would listen to music and sing along for hours.

One day she met a girl named Chara in the building, who was also a classmate in school, and they became fast friends. She invited Rapunzel over to her apartment to do homework together and her parents gave her permission to go over. One day Chara invited her over after school but forgot that her mother was taking her to the shopping mall to purchase some clothes. Rapunzel went to Chara's apartment, knocked on the door and Chara's father answered the door. He invited her in and told her that Chara would be back shortly. He sat on the couch beside her and began to rub her shoulders. He stroked her hair and told her how beautiful it was. He then proceeded to touch her in other places. Her mind was reeling in shock. All she could think was, "I have to get out of here." She stood up to run, but her knees gave away because she was frightened. He started toward her, and she mustered every ounce of strength she had, got up and ran out the door.

She went into her apartment and cried uncontrollably, but no one was around to console her. She cut off all of her hair, showered and dressed for bed. She stayed in her room and pretended to be asleep when her parents came home. She felt dirty and ashamed and didn't want anyone to look at her. She felt sad, depressed, and fearful. Her parents were concerned about the drastic change in her appearance. When they questioned her, she told them she wanted to try something new with her hairstyle. She avoided her friend Chara for the next eight months. She never told anyone what happened. She excelled in all of her classes and kept to herself. She graduated with honors and received a full scholarship to the university in that city.

One day, she felt as if someone was watching her. She looked around and saw the most beautiful smile that she had ever seen. It belonged to a very handsome classmate. He approached her and said that the sun was shining on her hair and she was beautiful. He then asked if they could go to the study hall to do homework together. At the mention of the word homework, she completely fell apart and stumbled blindly down the hall trying to escape the building as fast as she could. She arrived home, locked herself in her room and stayed there unable to eat, drink or function properly.

Meanwhile, the young man contacted the office of the university with his concern about what happened, and after a couple of days, they reached her parents. Her parents were unable to get anything out of her, so they decided to get her psychological help. She was finally able to relay to someone the trauma that she experienced as a child. She was able to sort out her feelings with the help of the psychologist and started the process of the long road to healing. She went back to the university and established a friendship with the nice young man that she met before. They fell in love and graduated at the same time. They got married and lived happily ever after.

The End

In this story, Rapunzel could represent the millions of people who have gotten trapped in life. They seem unable to find the right environment, people, or circumstances that make their lives more productive or pleasant. They're trapped behind walls of fear with beautiful songs in their hearts that'll never be heard by others. Perhaps they weren't the cause of this isolation.

Rapunzel was captured by her parents' decisions. She was stuck in the tall building singing to herself, without companions to talk to because she was unapproachable. She was hard to reach because she was guarded with her emotions. Her pain goes more in-depth than most because she pushes it down instead of pushing it out. She won't allow you in her space because she has been alone so long that she uses her solitude as a comfort zone. She has beautiful qualities, a beautiful voice, and beautiful hair but, was stuck with an "out of sight out of mind" mentality. She decided that it was safer in the tall building. No one could hurt her or mistreat her because she had the only means of access. She refused to be vulnerable again. It was safer to deny access than to experience rejection, betrayal, heartache or pain. Oh Rapunzel, Rapunzel! Let down your hair! Allow the Prince of Peace access to those emotional hurts that are buried just beneath the surface. In order for the pain to heal, it needs to be revealed.

Possible Characteristics of the Rapunzel Syndrome:

- may have a victim mentality
- may become paranoid
- may not trust people
- may not make friends easily
- may always be on the defensive
- may be emotionally inaccessible

The story of Jephthah's daughter is similar to this fairytale.

Judges 11:30-35

30 And Jephthah vowed a vow unto the LORD, and said, If thou shalt without fail deliver the children of Ammon into mine hands, 31 Then it shall be, that whatsoever cometh forth of the doors of my house to meet me, when I return in peace from the children of Ammon, shall surely be the LORD's, and I will offer it up for a burnt offering. 32 So Jephthah passed over unto the children of Ammon to fight against them, and the LORD delivered *them into his hands. ³³ And he smote them from Aroer, even till thou come to Minnith, even twenty cities, and unto the plain of the vineyards, with a very great slaughter. Thus the children of Ammon were subdued before the children of Israel. ³⁴ And Jephthah came to Mizpeh unto his house, and, behold, his daughter came out to meet him with timbrels and with dances: and she was his only child; beside her, he had neither son nor daughter. ³⁵ And it came to pass, when he saw her, that he rent his clothes, and said, Alas, my daughter! Thou hast brought me very low, and thou art one of them that trouble me: for I have opened my mouth unto the LORD, and I cannot go back.*

Jephthah made a rash vow to the Lord that if he was victorious in the battle against the children of Ammon, when he returned home, he would offer to God a sacrifice of the first thing that met him upon his return. It was a sad day when he returned, and his only child ran out to him with a heart full of joy. She loved her father and was devastated that he had made a promise to God to sacrifice her life. She would never marry or have children. She went to the mountains to mourn and went down in history as a person who was wronged in life. I thought it was fascinating that she displayed some of **the same qualities as Rapunzel:**

- She was beautiful
- She didn't complain about her lot in life
- She sacrificed herself for the convenience of others
- She turned her emotions inwardly or goes to a high place to express them
- She was untouchable

- She became accustomed to being isolated
- She didn't expect to be rescued

The last characteristic is a huge problem because if you don't expect to be free, you'll stay in bondage. These ladies knew they were treated unfairly. They never questioned the treatment or addressed the continuous results that occurred afterward. I believe they should have stood up for themselves once they reached the age of maturity. I don't believe anyone should remain stuck in a pattern of behavior just because that is the way they previously behaved. Rapunzel finally let down her hair and she experienced the happiness that she deserved. Jephthah's daughter remained in the shadow of her father's mistake.

I want to encourage anyone who has been taken hostage by their past to acknowledge the problem. Stop making excuses about why it is difficult to be free. God has the power to deliver you from every situation and bondage. There is nothing too hard for Him. He holds your future in His hands, but you have to allow Him access. Your voice needs to be heard among people, not in mountains, caves, or tall buildings. Sing unto the Lord a new song. Sing songs of deliverance, songs of praise, and songs of freedom. Be confident in your ability to become the beautiful person that you're destined to be. Stop mourning the past and live in the now. The future is bright if you choose to come out of the tower. It is time to proclaim your freedom. Be determined to open your heart to the lover of your soul and declare, "access granted."

Prayer

Father, I thank You that You're the Lord of breakthrough. I know that life has sometimes been unfair, but You're always just and merciful. God, I pray that our latter days will be far greater than our former days. I pray that You'll strengthen Your people as we live a life of freedom and abundance. Be glorified in us. Amen

Healing Prompt

Allow yourself to heal from trauma, pain and unjust treatment. Know that you're valuable and well-loved by the God of grace. He's able to restore your confidence in yourself. Love yourself enough to keep moving. Seek the help of others if you need to. Don't isolate yourself.

CHAPTER SEVEN

The Cinderella Syndrome

Romans 8:28

*And we know that all things work together for good to them that
love God, to them who are the called according to His purpose.*

The tale of Cinderella is about a young lady with a cruel stepmother who favors her daughters and mistreats Cinderella. The young stepdaughter is aided by a good fairy in her quest to attend an annual ball. She meets a prince there who has to seek her out after she hurriedly leaves the ball. He finds her by inquiring about a glass slipper that falls from her feet in her hasty departure. He travels throughout the kingdom, searching for the maiden whose foot fits the slipper. He finds her, asks her to marry him and they live happily ever after.

Cinderella

Once upon a time, there was a lovely young lady named Cinderella. She was loving, kind and well mannered. She lived with her father who was a software developer. As a single father, he would often invite her to his company to explore the vast field of technology. She developed a love for developing video games. They would often travel internationally to attend trade shows. She enjoyed meeting new people and learning new things immensely. On one trip to a foreign land, her father struck up a friendship with a single lady with two daughters close to Cinderella's age. They continued communication online and eventually married each other. He moved his new family into his home.

They knew that blended families took some adjustments on everyone's part. Their living situation started awkwardly and turned into a nightmare. The stepmother and her daughters couldn't adjust to the culture, the food or the environment. While the father was at work, Cinderella was mercilessly tormented, verbally attacked by her new family. She was miserable and no longer went to the office with her father because he wouldn't allow her to. He spent long hours at the office because of the tension in his home that was even leading to fights with his new wife.

One day while traveling overseas to a trade show, he met a kind young man who was also a software developer. He conversed with the young man and learned that he developed sports games. It instantly reminded him of his daughter who loved to tinker with software for games. He casually mentioned his daughter's passion and interest in games. The young man perked up and asked to meet his daughter. He informed the father about his startup company that was taking off and he was looking for fresh ideas as well as new eyes. Everyone that worked in his company was seasoned developers. He thought a fresh perspective would give him an edge. The father agreed to talk to Cinderella about meeting him. He returned home and found his family situation even worse than before. His wife and new daughters were resentful and bitter towards him and his daughter. He decided that he would call it quits and asked if they would be happier returning to their native country. They agreed on a financial settlement, divorced and moved back to their country.

His relationship with Cinderella wasn't the same. She avoided him and kept to herself. She was miserable. One day as he prepared for a trip, he remembered his promise to the young man on his last tour. He told Cinderella about their conversation and asked if she was interested in going. She showed interest in the opportunity to talk about her love for developing game software. They arrived at the trade show where she met the young man whose company had just ranked the number one company in the world. Her father introduced them, and there was an instant mutual attraction. They talked for hours and wanted to continue sharing. They continued talking every day of the trade show. Finally, the day came when it was time to return home. The young man knew that he was in love with Cinderella and didn't want her to leave. She was attracted to him but was hesitant to trust her heart because of the trauma that she experienced before. They continued to date online as well as meet several times a year. She fell deeply in love and entirely surrendered her heart to him. He asked her to marry him, she accepted, and they lived happily ever after.

The End

The Cinderella story is probably the story that millions of people can identify with. It is a heart-wrenching tale of unexpected change, hopelessness and unjust treatment. A wicked stepmother and stepsisters mistreated Cinderella but it could have just as easily been a corrupt system, turbulent times or misguided loyalty. Some people have been under oppression for so long that it causes them to adapt to their circumstances. They feel as if they have been down so long, there's no possibility of getting up. People adjust to poverty, sickness or disease too readily if they're operating under a Cinderella Syndrome. They adapt to the pain because it is familiar. They lose hope and never expect change.

They may miss opportunities for change because of their expectations. If you listen carefully, you'll hear a sigh of resignation. It sounds like: 'I'm always mistreated…' 'I'm the last person to be asked to social functions…' 'I don't have the right clothes, the right car…' 'I live in the wrong neighborhood.' Cinderella found herself in a bad situation through no fault of her own, but she had the opportunity to make the best of a bad situation through her thoughts, if not her actions. She could have prepared herself for a change in her position by believing that it could happen. She was sad and discouraged although her chance for happiness was so close. We sabotage our success when our expectations are low. We can't imagine that God wants to do something grand for us and are often caught up in a system that imposes limitations on us.

When Cinderella finally married the love of her life, she had to take the opportunity to forget all of the negative things that she endured. She had to consciously decide that a new beginning needed to connect with new thoughts so new ideas could emerge. She had to accept her husband's love and reject the fear of change. According to scripture, we don't even know what God has planned for us (1 Corinthians 2:9).

He has made promises to those who love Him. He's a covenant keeper. God promised the children of Israel that they would always have a remnant in the earth. When a decree from an earthly king went out to challenge that word, God reached down into the earth and pulled a little handmaiden out of an obscure location to save His people. We can find this story in the book of Esther.

Esther was an orphan who was raised by her cousin Mordecai. He loved her as if she was his daughter, she loved and honored him also. They were part of a Jewish remnant left subject to a pagan king. Esther came to the palace through unusual circumstances. She didn't expect to be taken to the castle and certainly never dreamed of being placed in the position of queen. She displayed **Characteristics of the Cinderella Syndrome, which are:**

- Doesn't recognize the favor upon one's life, can only see the present circumstances
- May have a stepchild mentality (feels less than)
- Low maintenance (didn't require anything to prepare her for the king)
- Low expectations (didn't expect the king to call her back into his presence)

- Forced into obscurity by circumstances (couldn't tell of her Jewish descent)
- May put others before themselves (so accustomed to serving others)

However, circumstances forced her to rise to her status as queen and ask to see the king when she found out that a decree was given by the king to destroy her entire race. Mordecai sent a copy of the decree to Esther and implored her to save her people (Esther 4:8-16).

Esther was terrified because she had been in the palace long enough to know the laws of the kingdom. She knew she could be put to death and she feared losing her life. Mordecai didn't give her a pass but insisted that she put her life on the line for her people. She was conditioned to putting others first, so she decided that she would go to see the king although it could cost her life. Spiritually, we have to be willing to die to the flesh to come into the presence of our King. We have to forget all of the hardships and trials that we have experienced and expect to see a brighter day. We have to believe that we're highly favored with a kingdom mentality. There aren't orphans or stepchildren in the kingdom. The Bible says that we're the sons of God. There are individual rights that accompany sonship. We can go to the Father without fear of rejection. We have a right to boldly approach the throne of grace that we may obtain mercy, and find grace to help in time of need.

The Kingdom of God is within us. If we're going to be used as Esther was, we must stop acting as if we don't belong at the ball or in the palace. We must go, and when we arrive, we must represent our King of kings and Prince of Peace. We expect to be seen and heard. We aren't running out of our shoes because our feet are shod with the preparation of the gospel. We'll move throughout the kingdom declaring that God's will be done on earth as it is in heaven.

Prayer

Father, I thank You that You said we should come boldly unto the throne of grace that we may find help in the time of need. We need the world to know that You're King of kings and Lord of lords. We purpose in our hearts to become kingdom citizens with the full rights that accompany that status.

Healing prompt

Believe in your heart that every stepchild has an opportunity to step out of their situation and into their destiny. If you can step out, you can step up!

CHAPTER EIGHT

Jack and the Magic Beans

Matthew 6:33

But seek ye first the kingdom of God, and His righteousness,
and all these things shall be added unto you.

The original tale of Jack is about a young man who trades his mother's cow for magic beans. His mother becomes angry and throws the beans out the window. They grow into a gigantic beanstalk that Jack climbs and meets a wealthy giant in a castle. He steals the giant's treasures which includes a goose that lays a golden egg. The giant chases him and Jack cuts down the beanstalk, thereby destroying the giant.

MY VERSION

Jack and the Magic Seeds

Once upon a time, a single mother was living in a rural area that didn't have many job opportunities. She had a teenage son named Jack. She worked long hours doing various jobs such as assisting the elderly, driving people to different places and babysitting. Jack went to school, went home to an empty house, and entertained himself with long hours of watching television and playing video games. Jack's mother contracted the flu and had to remain at home in bed for several weeks. She couldn't work, or pay her bills and they began to pile up, which made her worry. She realized that the only thing she had of monetary value was her car. She called Jack to her bedside and instructed him to take the car to a used car lot and sell it. She knew that Jack took driver's education in school but didn't have a license to drive, but she was desperate and felt that this was her only option. She gave Jack the keys, and he left to sell the car.

On his way to sell the car, he spotted four men standing on a corner. They appeared to be only a couple of years older than himself.

He stopped to ask for directions, and they asked him what he needed. He explained his mission and they told him that they had a better plan. They showed him some magic seeds and said to him that those seeds could bring him great wealth if he planted them in the right ground. He exchanged his mother's car for the magic seeds. He went back home and told his mother what happened. She was furious and told him to return the seeds and reclaim the car. Jack convinced himself that he could become wealthy by planting those seeds and decided to keep them. He left home and looked for the perfect ground to plant the seeds. Every time he found the right place, someone else came along and said that the spot was theirs. It happened so frequently that friction, chaos, and violence broke out in the little town.

Meanwhile, Jack's poor mother began to hear rumors of her dear son's plight. She borrowed enough money to catch a bus to the last place that he was spotted. When she got there, she met some young men standing on the corner who told her that Jack had gotten in trouble with the police and was downtown in jail. She didn't have enough money to get downtown and told them so. They offered to give her the bus fare, which was accepted gratefully. She offered to pay them back when she got back on her feet, but they declined the offer. His mother caught the bus downtown to the courthouse and requested information about Jack. They told her that he was awaiting trial.

She informed them that she didn't have money for his bail. She was overwhelmed with sadness at the dismal prospects. She began to blame herself for Jack's plight. She thought about all of the times she left him alone while she worked long hours. She thought about her decision to send him to sell the car. She began to weep and ran to the ladies' room. She continued to cry as other ladies came and went.

Finally, she heard a familiar voice calling her name. She looked up to see one of her former employers, who asked her why she was crying. She explained what happened to Jack and why she was crying. After pulling herself together, she asked the lady how her mother was. She had previously assisted her mother in her home after a bad fall. The former employer informed her that her mother passed away and that she was now back on her job as a full-time attorney in the courthouse. She told her that she would be willing to help Jack and also employ her full time as an office assistant with good pay. Jack's mother was so overwhelmed with joy and relief that she began to weep again. Jack was released on bond and returned to trial. The Judge gave him a chance to do community service. His mother started to work at the courthouse. During her lunch breaks and spare time, she began to give wise counsel to the youths that came in and out of the courthouse each day. She and Jack lived a peaceful, quiet life together until he got married and moved away.

The End

Jack is like millions of people around the world. He was born into a situation that caused him to always experience lack. He didn't have beautiful clothes, fancy cars or a luxurious home. Jack's mother was the sole provider of the family. She had a steady source of income but needed a car to get to work. Like so many others living below the poverty level, she was just one sickness away from being destitute. She still needed to provide food and shelter for her only child. I imagine the pain of being unable to feed, clothe and nourish my child would be unbearable. This story isn't so much about the mother as it is about Jack. There are plenty of mothers out there in the world who barely make ends meet. They struggle and do everything possible to provide for their families. They make great sacrifices and hard choices, but they keep going. They decide to do whatever it takes to have a better life. They aren't strangers to hard work, long days and longer nights. They forego food so their kids can eat. The mother in the story did her part in trying to make a home for Jack. She instructed him to take the car to the used car dealership to sell it, and that was when the trouble started. Jack met a young man with supposedly magic seeds. Jack was the prime target for a hustler or swindler. Their circumstances prime most people that are duped by con artists. They either lack something, have a poverty mentality, or are just plain greedy. Jack falls for the trick and exchanges the car for the seeds. I saw this story in the Bible on two occasions:

Genesis 25:29-34

29 And Jacob sod pottage: and Esau came from the field, and he was faint: 30 And Esau said to Jacob, Feed me, I pray thee, with that same red pottage; for I am faint: therefore was his name called Edom. 31 And Jacob said, Sell me this day thy birthright. 32 And Esau said, Behold, I am at the point to die: and what profit shall this birthright do to me? 33 And Jacob said, Swear to me this day, and he sware unto him: and he sold his birthright unto Jacob. 34 Then Jacob gave Esau bread and pottage of lentils; and he did eat and drink, and rose up, and went his way: thus Esau despised his birthright.

The eldest son Esau gave up his inheritance for a bowl of beans. As a firstborn son, Esau had the right to inherit the position of patriarch after his father's death. He also should have received a double portion of the family's wealth. Esau valued his comfort more than his birthright. He didn't want to experience hunger pains, and that's why he approached his brother Jacob. He wanted a quick fix for his problem, just like Jack in the fairy tale. People who always search for instant gratification will find themselves with temporary fixes. They'll discover that there is a price to pay for taking shortcuts. Jack and Esau were willing to do anything to get what they wanted. Esau didn't seem to care that his children were going to be affected by his decision to give up his birthright. These stories remain relevant. We observe people selling drugs, trafficking human beings and becoming lawless to get money. Money has become an idol, and human reasoning has replaced moral conscience.

Quick rich schemes have replaced work ethics. We have developed a selfish mentality. Society has shaped our worldviews exclusively. We tend to think there aren't absolutes and everything is subject to change. Jack and Esau made terrible decisions because of their desire to have something that they were lacking. Let's consider our choices in life and make decisions based on all of the facts. The facts are, a bowl of beans or magic seeds may cost far more than you're willing to pay.

The other story similar to Jack's: **Acts 8:9-24**

> *9 But there was a certain man, called Simon, which beforetime in the same city used sorcery, and bewitched the people of Samaria, giving out that himself was some great one: 10 To whom they all gave heed, from the least to the greatest, saying, This man is the great power of God. 11 And to him, they had regard, because that of a long time he had bewitched them with sorceries. 12 But when they believed Philip preaching the things concerning the kingdom of God, and the name of Jesus Christ, they were baptized, both men and women. 13 Then Simon himself believed also: and when he was baptized, he continued with Philip, and wondered, beholding the miracles and signs which were done. 14*

Now when the apostles which were at Jerusalem heard that Samaria had received the word of God, they sent unto them Peter and John: ¹⁵ Who, when they came down, prayed for them, that they might receive the Holy Ghost: ¹⁶ (For as yet he was fallen upon none of them: only they were baptized in the name of the Lord Jesus.) ¹⁷ Then laid they their hands on them, and they received the Holy Ghost. ¹⁸ And when Simon saw that through laying on of the apostles' hands the Holy Ghost was given, he offered them money, ¹⁹ Saying, Give me also this power, that on whomsoever I lay hands, he may receive the Holy Ghost. ²⁰ But Peter said unto him, Thy money perish with thee because thou hast thought that the gift of God might be purchased with money. ²¹ Thou hast neither part nor lot in this matter: for thy heart is not right in the sight of God. ²² Repent therefore of this thy wickedness, and pray God, if perhaps the thought of thine heart may be forgiven thee. ²³ For I perceive that thou art in the gall of bitterness, and in the bond of iniquity. ²⁴ Then answered Simon, and said, Pray ye to the Lord for me, that none of these things which ye have spoken come upon me.

Simon witnessed a higher power than he had ever experienced and decided that he needed to have that power. He assumed that all he had to do was offer enough money and he could operate in the power the Apostles were using. Simon didn't understand the spiritual implications of what he was witnessing. He just knew that if he could tap into that power, more people would seek him out to help them with their problems. He was a sorcerer, which meant that he was adept at practicing deceit. He didn't' intend to change even after he confessed that he believed the gospel. This created a problem for the Apostles because they knew that the gospel has the power to change your motives and intentions. Peter discerned although Simon was baptized, he hadn't been converted. His heart was still bound in iniquity. Simon's confession didn't lead to repentance. Therefore, he never changed. He wasn't interested in receiving the Holy Ghost as a gift for himself, but a tool to be used to impress others. Jack wanted magic beans in the fairytale and Simon wanted magical power in the real story.

The moral of this story concerning Jack, Esau, and Simon appears to be, the willingness to do anything to get what you want almost always leads to future trouble.

Possible Characteristics of the Jack and the Magic Seeds Syndrome:

- A constant yearning to have more or better
- A sense of entitlement
- Impulsive actions
- A desire to hold onto everything
- An inferiority complex
- Lack of motivation
- An impoverished mentality

Prayer

Father help us to understand that it is You that gives us the power to get wealth that You may establish Your covenant on the earth. Give us the wisdom to live within our means that we may have a peaceful and prosperous life. Amen.

Healing Prompt

Ask the Lord to show you how and by which means you may obtain wealth. When He shows you, act upon it with integrity. Power belongs to God and He's the only one that can give you true power.

CHAPTER NINE

Goldilocks

Psalm 24:1

The earth is the Lord's, and the fulness thereof;
the world, and they that dwell therein.

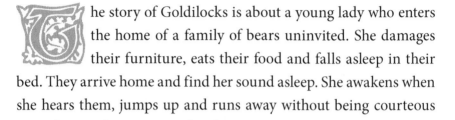

he story of Goldilocks is about a young lady who enters the home of a family of bears uninvited. She damages their furniture, eats their food and falls asleep in their bed. They arrive home and find her sound asleep. She awakens when she hears them, jumps up and runs away without being courteous enough to apologize or say thank you.

Goldilocks

nce upon a time, there was a young lady named Goldilocks. She was a high school junior with a restless spirit. She talked to the school counselors about her desire to quit school before her senior year. They tried to convince her to stay. She left school, ran away from home, and found herself in trouble. She stayed with friends who were always in trouble with law enforcement. They partied a lot and used illegal substances to make themselves feel good. One of her male friends asked her to take a cross country trip with him. She didn't know that he was carrying illegal substances in his car. The highway patrol stopped them, found narcotics, and took them to jail. She was frightened and alone. When the captain of the police found out that she was a minor, he felt compassion for her and released her into the custody of her parents. They wanted her to re-enroll back in school, but she refused and ran away again. She took some of their credit cards and caught a train to a large city.

Once again, Goldilocks was caught up with unsavory characters. She bought false identification and started barhopping with her friends. One night after a time of wild partying and drinking, one of her friends wouldn't wake up. They left their friend and called an ambulance from a public phone. They were afraid to stay and report what happened. They learned from a news report that their friend died from alcohol poisoning and that the police were looking for someone that could identify her, but no one came forward.

Goldilocks became increasingly anxious about finding a place to live. She wandered the streets for days feeling lost and confused. She was unhappy with her life, but she didn't know how to change it. She began to sleep on the sidewalks on top of a cardboard box. She thought about calling her parents, but she was too ashamed and too proud to ask for help.

One night, she laid her cardboard box down beside an elderly gentleman who was lying in an alley. They conversed and shared their life stories. He was a Vietnam veteran with Post-traumatic Stress Disorder. His daughter, who was a social worker, lived in the same city. She wanted him to stay with her, but he would have severe flashbacks and scare her kids. The man was unable to remain in any closed environment without anxiety or panic attacks. He advised Goldilocks to return to her parents, but she refused. They developed a friendship and watched out for each other. They rummaged through dumpsters behind restaurants to find food to share. One day, his daughter came to visit and bring him fresh clothes. He introduced her to Goldilocks. When she prepared to leave, he pulled his daughter aside to ask if she would try to help the young girl have a better life. His daughter promised that she would see what she could do. She began to visit her father regularly and would always bring clothes and food for both of them. She gained the trust of the young lady and asked if she wanted to visit her home for a nice warm shower and dinner. Goldilocks accepted her offer.

She repeated that process at least once a week for the following two months.

Finally, she asked Goldilocks if she would consider living with her and completing her education online. Goldilocks agreed. She moved in, and the social worker discovered that Goldilocks had always wanted to become a hairstylist. The social worker began to research schools in the area and realized that there was one within walking distance of her home. She didn't have the money to send Goldilocks to school so, she researched scholarships. In the meantime, she continued to update her father on Goldilocks' progress. She told her father about the cosmetology school and its fees. He informed his daughter that he had Veteran's benefits that were never received because he didn't have an address that they could send his checks to. His daughter went with him to the Veterans' Administration, completed the documents, and began collecting more than enough to pay Goldilocks' tuition. Goldilocks completed high school online, completed cosmetology school and opened a salon. The salon was successful because of its location and her astute business skills. She contacted her parents, who came to visit and were very happy to see her. Life continued to be successful for Goldilocks.

The End

This is a familiar story of a young lady's venture into the real world. During our course of life, we make decisions that not only affect our lives, but affect others' also. We were never told what Goldilocks' upbringing entails, but we know that she left home of her own free will. If she were from a stable, loving environment within a protective, caring family, she surely would have been warned about the dangers of the world.

I remember the saying "it's a jungle out there." Many times, parents, grandparents, aunts, and uncles try to keep their young loved ones within reach of the covering of a protective family. In the story, Goldilocks has no particular path in which she chose to go; she just wandered into life. She didn't consider the dangers of darkness approaching or other hostile forces. She wasn't sensitive to the sights or the sounds of life.

Goldilocks symbolizes those that have just wandered into life without directions or expectations. These types of people assume that the situations they find themselves in will be to their liking. When Goldilocks' meet challenges, they move on to something easier. When they encounter cushy jobs, cushy relationships, etc., they become bored quickly because it has to be just right. They may not realize that just right is still not perfect. Goldilocks' actions reveal her character. We can't go through life without any direction or awareness that what we do may affect others. Goldilocks ran away when she was about to be confronted. She had no intention of facing any consequences.

Fortunately, Jesus met a Goldilocks in the scriptures and set her life on course:

The Woman at the Well (John 4:6-10)

6 Now Jacob's well was there. Jesus, therefore, being wearied with his journey, sat thus on the well: and it was about the sixth hour. 7 There cometh a woman of Samaria to draw water: Jesus saith unto her, Give me to drink. 8 (For his disciples were gone away unto the city to buy meat.) 9 Then saith the woman of Samaria unto him, How is it that thou, being a Jew, askest drink of me, which am a woman of Samaria? For the Jews have no dealings with the Samaritans. 10 Jesus answered and

said unto her, If thou knewest the gift of God, and who
it is that saith to thee, Give me to drink; thou wouldest
have asked of him, and he would have given thee living
water.

The Samaritan woman experienced a life of continually seeking love, acceptance and a family. She married each man with the potential to give her what she wanted. The problem was that she may have expected them to satisfy her basic human need for unconditional love, which can only be given from our Creator, God. She tested everyone's heart that came into her life. I imagine that she couldn't find a perfect heart. Jesus told the Samaritan woman that she didn't know what or whom she was seeking. He explained to the woman that she had to properly position herself for a relationship with the Father. Jesus taught that nothing else would satisfy the thirst that she was experiencing. He confronted her inner drive to search for true love in the forest of life where men are seen as trees. Jesus knew He was the way, the Truth, and the Life and could reveal the truth to her concerning her life (see James 1:5).

Possible Characteristics of the Goldilocks Syndrome:

- May be a perfectionist
- May be unable to sustain meaningful relationships
- Perhaps distrustful of others
- May regularly run away from stressful situations

Prayer

Father, I thank you that You're ever-present as we travel through this world. We need Your wisdom, Lord. All we have to do is call upon

You, and You'll answer and show us great and mighty things. You uphold us with Your right hand, and we're ever so grateful to be a part of Your kingdom. I pray that Your will be done in our lives. Amen.

Healing Prompt

Forgive yourself and others for any mistakes of the past and go into your future with a new mindset.

CHAPTER 10

The Princess and the Frog

2 Corinthians 3:18

But we all, with open face beholding as in a glass the glory of the Lord, are changed into the same image from glory to glory, even as by the Spirit of the Lord.

he tale of the Princess and the frog is about a young princess who was playing alone and dropped her ball into a pond. A prince who was turned into a frog lived in the pond, saw her dilemma and offered to assist her in retrieving the ball. The only way to return to his natural state was if he was kissed by a lovely princess. He struck a bargain with her to exchange the ball for a kiss. Although it was difficult for her to keep her promise, she eventually kissed him and he turned into a prince. He married her and they lived happily ever after.

MY VERSION

The Princess and the Frog

nce upon a time, it was a beautiful Spring day. The flowers were budding and releasing an aroma in the air that was simply heavenly. It was the perfect setting for a perfect couple to join together in holy matrimony. The kiss of the sun graced the garden and the gazebo. The couple, who exchanged wedding vows were Mr. and Mrs. Smith. Mrs. Smith was the daughter of a prominent astronaut. She was pampered by her father and always saw the world through rose-colored glasses. Her parents went all out in making sure her wedding was perfect. They spared no expenses. Mr. Smith was a low-key college professor who adored his socialite wife. She was aloof and unapproachable to others, but warmly affectionate toward him. They confessed their love for each other on a daily basis.

After the ceremony and reception, they headed off into the sunset to enjoy a seven-day honeymoon. They cruised to Aruba, disembarked and went on a sightseeing tour. They toured quaint little villages, taking in the sights of architectural designs that were antiquated. They were in love with life, the island, and each other. They took a taxi to the nightclub district and enjoyed great music by the local bands. The night was perfect. As they were headed back to the ship, trying to hail a taxi, one of the patrons from the night club came out and saw their dilemma. He asked if they needed a ride. It was late, and they were ready to go back to the ship. The man appeared to be sober, well-mannered, and friendly, so they said yes. He dropped them off at the ship and went on his way.

Early the next morning as the ship prepared to leave the port, the Smiths heard a series of sirens. They then heard a voice on a megaphone asking the ship captain's permission to come aboard. The town's police captain and his officers boarded the ship. They explained that a nightclub patron was murdered the night before and was last seen with Mr. Smith. They identified him as the suspect that was on camera talking to the victim. The police took the Smiths to the police station and interrogated them. They showed them the victim's picture, and the Smiths confirmed that he gave them a ride to the ship. Mr. Smith was then arrested for murder and the authorities proceeded to investigate the crime. Mrs. Smith thought that they would find out that her husband's arrest was a mistake, so she stayed at the police station that day while the cruise ship went on to its next destination.

After two days, they told her she had to leave the station, alone. She was devastated and called home to share the tragic news with her parents. Meanwhile, her husband remained in jail without bond because he was a foreigner and they couldn't risk him leaving. He remained incarcerated for two years before they had a trial. He was convicted and sentenced to eighty years in prison. Mrs. Smith's life fell apart, and she went into a deep depression. She hardly ate or slept.

She needed assistance with her daily routine of getting out of bed and getting dressed. Her mother was able to help her for years until her own health began to fail.

She seemed to come out of the fog she was living in when her mother fell ill. She found a reputable Christian counselor who helped her through the process of emotional healing. She gradually became better and decided that she needed to bring closure to the relationship that never had a chance to grow or flourish. It'd been fifteen years since her husband had been incarcerated. She didn't think she was strong enough to continue waiting for a lifetime to fulfill her wedding vows. She wrote to him and shared her thoughts, heart and, regrets that they never got a chance to know each other as husband and wife. She wanted out of the marriage and told him so. He wrote back and told her that he understood and just had one request. He asked if she would visit one last time before she moved on with her life.

She went to visit him, but he didn't want to talk much. He looked lovingly into her eyes and took in every detail of her beautiful face and requested a goodbye kiss. She thought to herself that it would be like kissing a stranger. She leaned in to lightly touch her lips to his and all the love she felt for him immediately rushed to the surface. She felt as if her heart was going to burst. She embraced him with every ounce of her strength. She knew then, that no matter what happened, she was connected to him for life. She expressed all of her love and loyalty with that one kiss. She also released all of the horrible memories and pain with that one kiss. Every negative emotion began to fade with that one kiss. She kissed her husband until freedom washed up on the shores of her heart and his. She kissed him until the unshed tears disappeared. She kissed him until the unjust treatment, bitterness, and shock found its way to relief. One kiss and she was free. She was free to love, free to live, but most of all, she was free to hope again. Mrs. Smith left with a new-found determination to solicit help to prove his innocence. She researched and found an organization that handled wrongful conviction cases. They listened to her story and decided to take the case.

Two years later, the officials in Aruba found the true killer. They released Mr. Smith and compensated him for his time spent in their custody. The officials offered the Smiths a complimentary honeymoon, but they left the island on the first available flight after his release. Instead, they considered every day of their life together as a honeymoon. They went home and celebrated with their friends and family. They lived happily ever after.

This story unfolds as a tale of expectations. The young princess fell in love with a prince and expected to have a ball in life until she was met with a situation that she couldn't control. Most marriages begin with wonderful expectations from the couple, their families and friends. Everyone seems to accept the fact that marriages have their turbulent times. No one expects a spouse to jump ship at the first sign of trouble, but it occasionally happens. As situations arise, each person has to know their breaking point. What may be a deal-breaker for one person, may simply be a major inconvenience for someone else. Mrs. Smith made her decision after a long hard struggle, but her heart decided the final fate of the marriage.

I found a similar story in the Bible:

David and Michal (1 Samuel 18:20)

The princess Michal loved David until she didn't. She loved the status of having a man that everyone admired. She loved the glitter and glamor of the royal life. What she didn't enjoy was David leaping around like a frog prince while everyone watching. She loved the appearance of having it all together. She loved the recognition as a princess and a queen. Michal's disdain for a king that could act like and relate to the ordinary people was just too much for her genteel senses. Tragically, she despised him in the end (1 Samuel, 18:27; 2 Samuel 6:16).

I wish this story had a better ending, but it wasn't to be. Michal had a Princess Syndrome. She was used to always having her way. She knew who she was and what she had to offer any suitor who endeavored to pursue her. She was actually the first one in this relationship to make her feelings known. She knew that Her father had the ability to make something happen. He did and everything went well until David became King and didn't act as her father. She despised his disposition and his affinity for being with the people and worshipping God in public. The fact is, he was doing just that when she first met him. Each of the ladies in these two stories started out with the Princess Syndrome, but only one of them was willing to change.

Possible Characteristics of the Princess Syndrome:

- May have a sense of entitlement
- May be unable to endure hardship
- May expect preferential treatment
- May be rude or arrogant
- May tend to use people

Prayer

Father help us to have the mind of Christ and to think about those things from above. Father examine our hearts, and if there's evil there, please remove it by creating in us a clean heart and renewing the right spirit. Thank You for the purging process. Amen.

Healing Prompt

Pray for a renewed mind and sincere love for others. Think of a time when you have made decisions based solely on your feelings, or how it affected you and not others.

CHAPTER ELEVEN

Beauty and the Beast

1 John 3:2

Beloved, now are we the sons of God, and it doth not yet appear what we shall be: but we know that, when he shall appear, we shall be like Him; for we shall see Him as He is.

he original Tale is about a father who has pledged his daughter to be married to a man-beast to whom no one else wants to be with. He allows her to visit her family although her absence causes him to fall sick to the point of death. Upon learning that he is dying, she returns and nurses him back to health. She agrees to marry him and it is discovered that an evil spell that has been cast upon him was broken because of her love. He's actually a handsome prince. They married and lived happily ever after.

Beauty and the Beast

nce upon a time, there was a beautiful young female entrepreneur. She traveled extensively for her business during the week. She was heavily involved in the activities of her church. She kept that pace for several years after graduating from a university. One summer she decided to take a vacation. She couldn't remember the last time that she had one. She went to the beach, checked into a hotel, and decided to take a nap. She was tired, but for some reason, she couldn't fall asleep. She got up and decided to take a stroll on the beach. She watched the waves roll in one after another, often overlapping, and thought to herself, what a beautiful ocean.

The beauty of the island was astonishing! She was perplexed as to why she never noticed the beauty of nature before. She went back to the room, showered and dressed for bed. She laid down with the beauty of that day flowing through her mind. She fell into a peaceful, relaxing sleep. She awoke the next morning feeling refreshed and alert, while still excited about what she experienced the day before. She dressed and went to the hotel's restaurant to eat breakfast.

While waiting for her food order, she looked around casually. There were mostly families in the dining room. She saw a child sitting on his father's lap while his mother nursed an infant. She looked at the door and saw a youth soccer group waiting to be seated. All of a sudden, she felt alone. She had never experienced loneliness before. She didn't recognize the feeling initially. She immediately began to experience a range of emotions. She saw herself busy with life but not living. She got up and left the restaurant to sort through her feelings. She went to the beach and immediately saw similar scenarios on the beach. She saw couples frolicking together. She saw parents chasing children. She watched seniors walk together with serene looks on their faces. She suddenly felt as if she had been in a time machine. She always believed that she would have a family of her own. She sat at the beach on a bench for hours allowing those thoughts to run through her mind.

Suddenly, she saw a middle-aged, well-dressed gentleman headed her way. He approached her and asked if she was okay. He explained that he was attending a business convention in the next hotel. He stated that he noticed her sitting there when he went in for the morning session. He was leaving the evening session and saw that she was still sitting there. He was concerned about her. She looked at him as if in a daze and said. "Yes, I'm okay." All of a sudden, she couldn't contain her emotions any longer and blurted out. "No, actually I'm not okay."

To her complete horror, she found herself blurting out all that she experienced over the past two days. He sat down and listened until she finished. He began to share his story with her. He was a recent divorcee whose marriage failed because of his total immersion in building a successful company. He achieved his goal in business but destroyed his marriage in the process. His wife wanted children, but he thought they should wait until a later time. She eventually gave up and asked for a divorce. He talked about his faith. He believed in God but wasn't able to fit daily devotions or weekly worship times into his schedule. He felt that he was missing out on life, but he didn't know how to do a course correction. They talked until the wee hours of the morning. They concluded that life could be a beauty or it could be a beast. They decided that it was all about perspective. They also wanted to continue talking and sharing. They chose to keep in touch.

They communicated via phone, internet, and occasional face-to-face meetings for two years. They agreed to hold each other accountable to take time to enjoy life. It wasn't an easy adjustment from total immersion in work, to occasionally relaxing, but they were determined. They created a plan to begin with one pleasurable activity per week. Although it was a small start, it was a good plan and they stuck with it.

During that process, they discovered their mutual honor and respect for each other. They allowed their feelings to deepen into a strong bond of love. They eventually married and lived happily ever after.

The End

This is indeed a love story. I'm not referring to the love between a man and a woman. I'm referring to a passion for life. I'm talking about living and enjoying people, places, and things. When we realize that this planet has lots of wonderful experiences to discover, we'll learn how to enjoy them. The couple in this story initially saw life as an opportunity for success. They didn't take their definitions of success into account. By all accounts of their conversation, there were huge successes in some areas and dismal failure in others. They failed to prioritize their goals in life and weren't able to see the effect their actions would have on others. They worked brutal schedules that took its toll on their bodies and mental health. Although this couple found that life can be a beast, they kept at it until things turned around for them.

This story ended so beautifully as fairy tales tend to, but I found a similar story in the Bible with a great but unexpected end.

> **Abigail and Nabal** (1 Samuel 25:3, 14, 21-23, 36-39)
>
> *³ Now the name of the man was Nabal, and the name of his wife Abigail: and she was a woman of good understanding, and of a beautiful countenance: but the man was churlish and evil in his doings, and he was of the house of Caleb. ¹⁴ But one of the young men told Abigail, Nabal's wife, saying, Behold, David sent messengers out of the wilderness to salute our master, and he railed on them. ²¹ Now David had said, Surely in vain have I kept all that this fellow hath in the wilderness so that nothing was missed of all that pertained unto him: and he hath requited me evil for good. ²² So and more also do God unto the enemies of David, if I leave of all that pertain to him by the morning light any that pisseth against the wall. ²³ And when Abigail saw David, she hasted, and lighted off the ass, and fell before David on her face, and bowed herself to the ground, ³⁵ So David received of her hand that which she had brought him, and said unto her, Go up in peace to thine house; see, I have hearkened to thy voice, and have accepted thy person. ³⁶ And Abigail*

came to Nabal; and, behold, he held a feast in his house, like the feast of a king; and Nabal's heart was merry within him, for he was very drunken: wherefore she told him nothing, less or more, until the morning light. ³⁷ But it came to pass in the morning when the wine was gone out of Nabal, and his wife had told him these things, that his heart died within him, and he became as a stone. ³⁸ And it came to pass about ten days after, that the Lord smote Nabal, that he died. ³⁹ And when David heard that Nabal was dead, he said, Blessed, be the Lord, that hath pleaded the cause of my reproach from the hand of Nabal, and hath kept his servant from evil: for the Lord hath returned the wickedness of Nabal upon his own head. And David sent and communed with Abigail, to take her to him to wife.

Abigail was married to a beast and had to intervene on his behalf to stop David from killing him and his household. I don't know how many times she had previously done this, but Nabal's servants seemed to know that she was the person that could handle the situation. The Bible says Abigail was "of a beautiful countenance and good understanding." She was the epitome of beauty and the beast because she had an understanding heart and wisdom to make improvements for her husband when he would lapse into his drunken stupors.

The contrast between the two was evident. He was foolish, but she was wise; he was beastly, but she was beautiful. The story ended with David taking Abigail to be his wife. She probably never dreamed that she would become a queen. That is indeed a fairytale ending (Ecclesiastes 3:11).

Characteristics of Beauty and the Beast Syndrome

- May be unable to appreciate the valuable things in life
- May have a hard time connecting with others
- May have a distorted view of the actions of others

Prayer

Father, I thank You for You know the plans You have to prosper us and not bring us harm. We bless You for Your faithfulness in establishing us in the ways of righteousness. We'll forever praise and adore You because You're the only true and living God. Be glorified in our lives. In Jesus' name, Amen.

Healing Prompt

Purpose in your heart that you'll take time to enjoy life and appreciate your loved ones.

CHAPTER TWELVE

The Boy Who Cried Wolf

Proverbs 19:1

Better is the poor that walketh in his integrity than he that is perverse in his lips and is a fool.

The original tale was about a young lad who was caring for the townspeople's flock and repeatedly pretended a wolf was trying to harm the flock. When an actual wolf appeared to attack the flock, he cried out for help but no one believed him. Therefore, the wolf was able to harm the flock.

The Boy Who Cried Wolf

Once upon a time, there was a young man from a wealthy family. His parents were local politicians grooming him to be a national political figure. He was allowed as a child to attend political meetings. He discovered the truth could be altered to get better results from attending those meetings. He also learned that some people lied outright if they felt they needed to. He was mentored in that area by some of his father's colleagues. No one challenged the lies and misdirected half-truths, so he felt they were okay. He completed his education as he developed a reputation as an upcoming bright, political figure. He followed the pattern of his mentors, resulting in a rise to power. He made false promises and smeared the names of his political opponents. He misused campaign funds and was never caught. He began to believe that he was invincible and involved foreign leaders into his web of deceit.

He never considered that some of those foreign leaders were even more astute at deception than he was. He quickly rose within the ranks of his fellow peers. He was considered a mover and shaker. Others sought him out when they needed a boost within their positions. He shared how to get ahead, but his knowledge came with a price tag attached to it.

Finally, he was accused of corruption and bribery of a foreign national official. He assumed that his name would be cleared in the investigation because he never had any contact whatsoever with that nation. No one believed him because, although everyone was suspicious of his activities, no one could prove anything. It turned out that there were twin brothers who were the heads of state in two different nations. He was involved with one of the brothers but not the other. There were photos and intel that were altered to build a case against him. He was arrested, tried and sent to prison.

The End

This is a familiar story about a person who continually tells untruths for whatever reason. We used to call it "crying wolf." The young politician was brilliant and could have possibly risen up in the ranks as a dynamic statesman; however, He chose to fabricate to advance his status in life. He cried wolf so many times, that when he spoke the truth, no one believed him.

Integrity is a desired characteristic of leadership. Some people don't seem to realize that they're lying because it's become a part of their character. I found a similar story in the Bible is the story of David and Goliath.

A great Philistine giant named Goliath that stood over nine feet tall came to the front of the Philistine battle line each day for forty days and mocked the Israelites and their God.

David and Goliath (1 Samuel 17:4, 8, 16, 33, 46)
⁴ And there went out a champion out of the camp of the Philistines, named Goliath, of Gath, whose height was six cubits and a span. ⁸ And he stood and cried unto the

armies of Israel, and said unto them, Why are ye come out to set your battle in array? Am not I a Philistine, and ye servants to Saul? Choose you a man for you, and let him come down to me. ¹⁶ And the Philistine drew near morning and evening and presented himself forty days. ³³ And Saul said to David, Thou art not able to go against this Philistine to fight with him: for thou art but a youth, and he a man of war from his youth. ⁴⁶ This day will the Lord deliver thee into mine hand, and I will smite thee, and take thine head from thee, and I will give the carcasses of the host of the Philistines this day unto the fowls of the air, and to the wild beasts of the earth; that all the earth may know that there is a God in Israel.

The giant Goliath was a man of war from his youth. He likely never experienced a significant defeat in his entire life. Goliath's sense of his ability to conquer any opposition was exaggerated. He probably doubted that he could be conquered. He cried wolf or in his case "Giant" for forty days. The Israelite army believed him, the citizens believed him, but more importantly, the King believed him! Imagine allowing an enemy to terrorize your people day after day. The days turned into weeks as Goliath strutted his stuff on the front line of the armies. He taunted, challenged and defied anyone to call his bluff.

Finally, David arrived on the scene and assessed the situation. After his assessment, David was sure that Goliath was wolfing. He slayed the giant that was threatening God's people. So many times, within the body of Christ, we forget to use discernment and accept anything we hear that sounds like it could be right. We should tell our fellow sisters and brothers that it isn't acceptable to cry wolf intentionally because there are real wolves that'll come in to devour the flock. Wolves come in several different forms. Some may be female, male, young or old. Shepherds are supposed to watch over the flock and will do well to recognize a wolf in disguise.

Possible Characteristics of Crying Wolf Syndrome

- May appear invincible
- May have a different perspective than most other people
- May fantasize frequently
- May be unable to differentiate between a lie and truth
- May embellish simple truths
- May have a vivid imagination
- May always seek attention

Prayer

Lord, I thank You that You are the Way, the Truth and the Life and no one comes to the Father except through You so we acknowledge this truth and ask You to help us walk in Your light. Amen

Healing Prompt

Ask the Lord to deliver you from every form of deception. Resist the temptation to be dishonest in any situation. Guard your heart and mind.

CHAPTER THIRTEEN

The Three Little Pigs

Psalm 127:1

Except the Lord build the house, they labour in vain that build it: except the Lord keep the city, the watchman waketh but in vain.

The original tale is about three little pigs heading out into the world to build their lives and their houses. They each choose different materials. One pig chooses straw and another chooses sticks to build their homes. The third pig uses bricks. A big, bad wolf blows down the stick and straw houses to attack the pigs. He isn't able to blow down the brick house because it is sturdy.

The Three Little Pigs

Once upon a time, on December 31st, on a cold wintery night, the staff at a regional hospital were waiting to see which baby would arrive first in the new year. At twelve twenty-two, a mother pig suddenly yelled out and pushed. Her first baby came out, but right behind him was another, and behind him was another. The triplets entered the world with a lot of fanfare, rejoicing, and jubilation. Their parents had an enormously difficult time conceiving and thought they would never be able to have children. They were elated to become parents! The staff showered the babies with gifts. The local media covered their story because they were the first triplets born in that region. Well-wishers sent cards, flowers, and gifts.

The little pigs grew up in a loving environment with their every whim indulged. They had cars and plenty of money in high school. They had plenty of friends, were very popular, matriculated college and set out to establish a life for themselves. The first pig built his life around casinos, lottery tickets and mostly games of chance. The second pig decided to partner with an unstable bull to open a business. The third pig was a conservative real estate investor who bought apartments, single-family homes, and vacant land.

One year, there was a downturn in the economy. Stock prices dropped. Foreclosures were rampant. People lost their jobs. It was a terrible time. The first little pig became homeless and destitute. The second little pig lost a lawsuit that was filed by his business partner. He lost his business and all of his assets including his home. Meanwhile, the third little pig began to buy several foreclosures at a fraction of their worth. He amassed an enormous amount of wealth. He also found his family members and helped them get back up on their feet. They realized that the decisions to build their lives in a haphazard manner caused them to become destitute in economic downtimes. However, because of their business savvy sibling, they all prospered.

The End

In this tale, the three little pigs were preparing to go out into the world to build a life and secure their futures. According to their story, they were youthful, probably energetic and as a bonus, they had a good head start in life. It appeared that the first thing they did was continue their privileged lifestyles. Each pig acted according to the standard that they had set for themselves. The first pig chose an easy but risky plan. The second pig chose a slightly better plan that still carried risks. The third pig seemed to have put much thought into the building process and decided that a sturdy structure was the way he wanted to build. I believe each one of them was satisfied until the testing time came. Life's struggles, storms, and surprises have a way of testing us. Along comes, a big bad problem and everything begins to crumble because there was only one pig with the foresight to prepare for unexpected adversity.

Unfortunately, almost all of us have experienced some failure in securing our futures through strategic planning. When I look back over my life, I realize that had I known what I know now through experience, I would certainly have made different choices. I understand that youth and lack of knowledge played a significant role in my preparation, but once I came into the knowledge of the truth, I should have acted accordingly. Fortunately, my story didn't end like the first two pigs because of the grace of God. I searched the scriptures for revelation on preparation for the future and found it in the book of Matthew.

Matthew 7:24-29

24 Therefore whosoever heareth these sayings of mine and doeth them; I will liken him unto a wise man, which built his house upon a rock: 25 And the rain descended, and the floods came, and the winds blew, and beat upon that house; and it fell not: for it was founded upon a rock. 26 And every one that heareth these sayings of mine, and doeth them not, shall be likened unto a foolish man, which built his house upon the sand: 27 And the rain descended, and the floods came, and the winds blew, and beat upon that house, and it fell: and great was the fall of it. 28 And it came to pass when Jesus had ended these sayings; the people were astonished at his doctrine: 29 For he taught them as one having authority, and not as the scribes.

Jesus acted just like the mother of the three little pigs. He admonished His disciples to be wise when dealing with the world. He taught them how to be fruit bearers and kingdom citizens. He told them that they were living stones (1 Peter 2:5).

Possible Characteristics of the Foolish Pig Syndrome:

- Doesn't take advice easily
- Doesn't plan for a rainy day
- Doesn't count the cost of taking shortcuts
- Walks in fear of losing possessions
- Doesn't discern dangerous situations

Prayer

Father, I thank You that You have called us into righteousness, peace, and joy as our portion. I thank You that in You there is no darkness at all, so we choose to walk in the light. Help us discern the enemies of our soul who continually endeavor to derail us. We decide to walk in the path of righteousness because Your word is a lamp unto our feet and a light unto our path. Amen.

Healing Prompt

Be willing to take wise advice and accept accountability for your actions.

CHAPTER FOURTEEN

The Grasshopper and the Ant

Proverbs 6:6

Go to the ant, thou sluggard; consider her ways, and be wise:

he original tale is about an ant who diligently works in the Summer to store up food for Winter. The grasshopper spends his time leisurely during the Summer while failing to prepare for Winter. He then begs the ant to give him food for the Winter which the ant refuses to do.

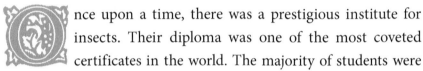 MY VERSION >

The Grasshopper and the Ants

nce upon a time, there was a prestigious institute for insects. Their diploma was one of the most coveted certificates in the world. The majority of students were incredibly talented, intelligent, -or artistic. They usually gravitated towards those students who had similar characteristics. The ants hung out with each other. The crickets hung out with crickets, and the grasshoppers hung out with grasshoppers. The culture of the grasshoppers was fun-loving activities, singing, dancing and being carefree. The ants, on the other hand, were hardworking, attentive and methodical. The crickets, however, could facilitate between the two extremes and do both.

The institute was known for having high performing graduates. Every major industry in the world tried to recruit them at the beginning of their senior year. The ants started researching during their spring break, and by the summer, they had gathered enough information to decide what offers they would entertain. They knew the positions to apply for, the salary they wanted and the locations they wanted. Meanwhile, the grasshoppers anticipated the spring break as an opportunity to take a trip abroad to sing with a well-known rock band. They approached the ants and asked if they wanted to travel with them for this once in a lifetime opportunity. The ants explained that it was their tradition to spend time preparing for career opportunities in the spring and summer before graduation.

The group of grasshoppers thought it was so hilarious that they joked and teased them mercilessly. They even made up a jingle about the ants: "*All work and no play will make the ants cray, cray.*" They would laugh hilariously at their own jokes. The grasshoppers then approached the crickets who also declined because they thought of themselves as an orchestra and thought that rock music was well below their standard. However, the grasshoppers didn't tease them for some reason.

The grasshoppers hopped on a plane for their destination and had a fantastic time. They rocked and rolled all week long and then rocked in the aircraft on their way back to the campus. The ants worked together diligently to find the top-rated companies in the world. They shared ideas, plans and assistance to others in their group who needed it. The crickets scurried through the halls, singing at the top of their voices. They enjoyed themselves tremendously. Senior year arrived and the institute sponsored a career fair. Major companies attended to scout for potential recruits. The ants already knew what the companies offered and were able to ask informed intelligent questions. The grasshoppers were asking questions of the ants instead of the company representatives. The Ants didn't have time to answer because they were busy taking notes that corresponded with what they already knew. The crickets just went from table to table picking up pamphlets and noisily discussing them among themselves. Graduation day arrived, and all of the students' families and friends were celebrating and asking about their future endeavors.

Most of the ants already had offers and told the less fortunate ones that they would put in a recommendation for them at their respective companies. The grasshoppers went to their homes and researched companies. The crickets scattered, each one with their own ventures. It was incredible that they all graduated with an average of 4.0 Grade Point Average.

The End

When you look at the diligence of the ants, you realize that a lot of people have Grasshopper Syndrome. It seems we should enjoy the fruits of our labor while the weather is clear. No one wants to work day after day without a chance to play. However, there is a time to work and a time to play. Preparation is never lost time. An old proverb says "make hay while it is day." Sometimes we have to delay instant gratification to get long-term results. It may not be easy, but it sure will be worth it.

We should consider the story in the Bible when Isaac had a supernatural intervention in the time of famine because he sowed seed at an inconvenient time (Genesis 26: 1-3, 12-13,)

Isaac didn't have a chance to sow seeds into the land of Gerar, but his father Abraham did. God told Isaac to sow where he was planted when hardship came upon the land. He sowed and received a hundredfold return within the same year. He needed the wisdom of God to prosper. God instructs us to consider the ants' ways of providing for themselves (Proverbs 6:6-11).

Possible characteristics of the Grasshopper Syndrome:

- May hop from job to job or idea to idea
- Doesn't lay aside anything for the future
- May be carefree
- May be oblivious to changing times
- Perhaps shortsighted

Prayer

Father, I thank You that Your word directs us to the industrious ant as an example of fruitfulness. We trust that You'll strengthen our hands for the work that You have called us to do.

Healing Prompt

Allow the Lord to lead you in your journey of life. Ask Him to free you from any fear of failure, procrastination or laziness.

The Tortoise and the Hare

1 Corinthians 9:24

[24] Know ye not that they which run in a race run all, but one receiveth the prize? So run, that ye may obtain.

here is a classic tale about a tortoise (turtle) and a hare (rabbit) who challenged each other to a race. The rabbit started out extremely fast as the turtle plodded along at a slow pace. The rabbit was so far ahead that he got distracted and veered off from the designated path. The turtle was slow but consistent and finished the race first.

The Tortoise and the Hare

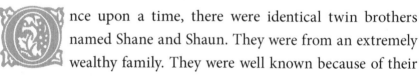nce upon a time, there were identical twin brothers named Shane and Shaun. They were from an extremely wealthy family. They were well known because of their parents' philanthropic activities. Everyone in their circles knew that Shane exhibited the social skills of his mother, who was an outgoing, talkative extrovert. Shaun's disposition was closer to his father, who was introverted and mild-mannered. They'd recently graduated from one of the top universities in the nation and were contemplating career choices. Shane earned his Juris Doctor degree but also had a Bachelor's in political science. He joined a prestigious law firm and was able to have valuable input in many of their major cases. He

became restless because he thought he'd chosen an exciting career, but realized each case took multiple years to litigate. The pace was much too slow for him. He decided to go into local politics with the idea that perhaps he could rise up in the ranks. He did so for several years and realized that politics wasn't for him. He continued to change careers until he reached retirement age. He never felt fulfilled or felt like he'd ever accomplished anything. He suddenly realized that he just drifted through life. He didn't have a family, except for his twin Shaun.

Shaun received his Master's degree in accounting. He joined an accounting firm and proceeded to move up in the firm slowly but steadily. He enjoyed what he did and he would miss the office upon retirement. However, the owner of his accounting firm was contemplating retirement and inquired about selling it. Everyone was astonished when they heard the news because they assumed they had quite a few years before that happened. Shaun immediately went into action. He discussed it with his attorneys and found that the transition would go smoothly if he chose to buy it. He purchased it and lived happily ever after.

The End

This story plays itself out in millions of lives. It is rare that people know exactly what they want in life at an early age. Our world views are shaped through the years of interacting with community, peers, family and others. We then begin to choose our paths of life and hope for the best. Things don't always work out as we feel they should. Life happens, so we must choose to continue even when we feel like giving up. Permanent failure shouldn't be an option. Just like the tortoise and the hare, our goal is to reach the desired destination. So, I want to encourage you to stay focused, don't compare yourself to others, stay in your lane and finish strong! The Bible also shares a classic tale of two sisters who wanted the same thing out of life and had to learn how to cope as they struggled to reach their goal (Genesis 29:16-18,).

These two young ladies' dreams and aspirations were centered on one major thing: they desired a loving husband and family. The elder sister, Leah, was slightly disadvantaged because she was older and not quite as beautiful as her younger sister. She yearned for a husband that would love, honor, protect and cherish her. It didn't happen on her timetable nor did it happen as she thought it should. Her father intervened for her and tricked Jacob into marrying her. I'm sure that her heart was wounded by the thought that Jacob preferred and loved her sister.

As was the custom in those days, Leah went along with the plot and settled into her destiny as an unloved, unwanted wife. Although it wasn't the best of circumstances, her status as the wife allowed her to at least have part of her dream come true as she proceeded to bear him children. Her story ends with her bearing Jacob seven children. The Bible says when the Lord saw that Leah was hated, He opened her womb, but Rachel was barren. She was fruitful in the marriage. It wasn't a perfect situation but she finally concluded that she should praise God for her fruitfulness (Genesis 29:35). She went down in history as a matriarch of Israel.

It was a story of love at first sight. Jacob saw Rachel at the well preparing to water her father's flock and instantly fell in love. He forgot his deception of his father in order to attain his brother's birthright. He forgot his brother's anger at his deception and his desire for revenge. He forgot his mother's fear that his brother would kill him. He forgot everything except the lovely woman coming towards the well that he was standing beside. He lifted up his voice and wept, not in pain, but in joy and pleasure. Jacob wept in relief that he found his uncle with such a beautiful daughter. He wept because once he saw her, the journey didn't quite seem as long and lonely anymore. He kissed her and his world became right again. He told her who he was and her world became unquestionably interesting.

Rachel had always longed for a strong handsome man to come into her life. She'd always longed for a family. They approached her father and were given permission to marry. Her father delayed their marriage with his deceptive, conniving ways. They were finally married and she discovered that she couldn't have children. Rachel was beautiful but barren. She longed for the sweet touch of a baby's face against her own. She wanted to hear the pitter-patter of tiny feet running through the house to find mommy. She longed to burp, bathe and cuddle her own child. Although Jacob loved Rachel tremendously, it wasn't enough. Each sister desired what the other one had. Finally, after many years of struggle, the Lord intervened once again for the sisters (Genesis 30:22-24) Rachael conceived and gave Jacob two sons.

I'm convinced that life can be compared to a race. When we start out, we may not know what is ahead of us but we should have a goal or destination in mind. Our pace may change, the direction may change or we may encounter obstacles but our main objective is to keep moving until we reach our destiny (1 Corinthians 9:24,).

Characteristics of the Tortoise and Hare (rabbit) Syndrome

- A slow and steady mentality
- Deliberate and focused
- May wander from place to place
- May always seem in a hurry
- May give up easily
- May be easily distracted
- May take shortcuts

Prayer

Father, I thank You that the steps of a good man are ordered by the Lord. I know that You delight when You see us going the right way. I ask You to illuminate our path and lead us into righteousness. Be our shield and protector as we journey through life. Uphold us with Your righteous right hand and preserve our way. Amen.

Healing Prompt

Keep moving! When life challenges you and your journey is difficult, keep moving!

CHAPTER FIFTEEN

Fascinating Tales

Deuteronomy 29:29

The secret things belong unto the Lord our God: but those things which are revealed belong unto us and to our children forever, that we may do all the words of this law.

At this point, I would like to shift from fairytales to fascinating tales. At the beginning of this book, I told you that fairytales are fantasy tales that aren't true, but one may gain some truths from them. In this context, fascinating tales are different. These tales are Biblical stories told in a simplistic manner. I remember reading the Bible as a child. We used a large-sized King James Bible as a coffee table decoration. I didn't understand much of what I read, but I was fascinated with some of the stories and their characters. I couldn't connect what I was learning to apply it to my life. I just got pleasure out of reading. I was intrigued and even imagined myself in the context of the stories. I knew that all of the stories I'd read had one central character who was sometimes called the God of Abraham, Isaac, and Jacob. He was also called other names, but faith in Him was the dominant theme. The Bible tells us of extraordinary stories of hope of men and women and exploits relevant to that faith in the book of Hebrews. God inspired the writer to give us a small glimpse into their world of heroism, triumph, and challenges (Hebrews 11:33-39).

All of the tales in the preceding scriptures are indeed fascinating! You can read a story from a book, or tell a bedtime tale to the kids you're babysitting. Tales can be real or fictional but are usually a narrative, with a beginning and an end - made more interesting and exciting with vivid details.

I continued to read the Bible into adulthood. I still didn't comprehend much of what I learned until I accepted Christ into my life. Then I began to understand as the Spirit revealed the scriptures to me (Deut 29:29). So, in light of that fact, I want to share a simple version of Bible stories. Perhaps there is a reader who can identify with my initial lack of understanding of the Bible.

The writer of Hebrews tells us about the fascinating characters of the Old testament. They're sometimes called "heroes of the faith". I totally agree with that summation but I also believe there were quite a few heroes in the New Testament. I want to share a few stories with you.

The Good Samaritan (Luke 10:30-37)

30 And Jesus answering said, A certain man went down from Jerusalem to Jericho, and fell among thieves, which stripped him of his raiment, and wounded him, and departed, leaving him half dead. 31 And by chance there came down a certain priest that way: and when he saw him, he passed by on the other side. 32 And likewise a Levite, when he was at the place, came and looked on him, and passed by on the other side. 33 But a certain Samaritan, as he journeyed, came where he was: and when he saw him, he had compassion on him, 34 And went to him, and bound up his wounds, pouring in oil and wine, and set him on his own beast, and brought him to an inn, and took care of him. 35 And on the morrow when he departed, he took out two pence, and gave them to the host, and said unto him, Take care of him; and whatsoever thou spendest more, when I come again, I will repay thee. 36 Which now of these three, thinkest thou, was neighbour unto him that fell among the thieves? 37 And he said, He that shewed mercy on him. Then said Jesus unto him, Go, and do thou likewise.

This story is all about care and compassion for others. Christ demonstrated this abundantly while He walked the earth. It was significant that two others from the religious community had an opportunity to assist the wounded man but chose not to. Perhaps it wasn't convenient. Maybe they thought he was beneath them. Our conscience and mercy toward humanity should compel us to be a blessing to someone other than our immediate loved ones. Jesus said you'll know His disciples by their love for one another. The stranger, who happened to be of another culture was willing to lay aside his differences and lend a helping hand.

MY VERSION

The Good Samaritan

Once upon a time, Bob and Jane were settling in their respective careers as a law enforcement officer and a flight attendant. Bob descended from a long line of military and law enforcement background. Jane was a free-spirited, lovable young lady who loved to travel. They met on an online dating site. Bob appeared to be charming and attentive. They fell in love and married. Jane wanted to continue her career as a flight attendant. Bob was moving up the ladder in his career and relocating wasn't an option for him. They decided that she would relocate to his area. With combined incomes, they were able to buy a nice condominium in an upscale neighborhood. Their neighbors were friendly and would occasionally gather for a barbecue in the common area.

One day a department investigation revealed that Bob had numerous unaddressed complaints. His supervisor was a close friend and never documented them. Over a dozen people complained of verbal and physical abuse at his hands. This was over a course of years. The investigators recommended he be placed on paid leave until they sorted things out. He decided not to tell Jane about the situation.

Meanwhile, Jane was thriving in her career and enjoying traveling. Bob told her that they should take a vacation before he received a promotion on his job. He felt that he would be extremely busy soon. Jane conceived while on vacation and only discovered it several weeks later. She was apprehensive about telling Bob because he had become withdrawn and moody. She resolved to gather her courage and tell him.

When she finally told him, it was as if he turned into another man. The once kind, loving and attentive Bob turned mean, sullen and abusive. He stated that she and the people on his job were trying to destroy him. He said, they never discussed having children and he didn't want any. He told her to get an abortion right away. She was shocked and confused as he raved like a mad man. She asked him what was going on at his job so, he told her. She tried to encourage him but was unable to.

Weeks passed as Jane continued working and taking extra flights to be away from home. The arguments and fights became so volatile that others in their building could plainly hear them. No one wanted to get involved as they knew that he was a law enforcement officer. There was an elderly neighbor who'd lost her only child in a domestic violence incident ten years previously. She tried to convince Jane to get help to no avail. One night, the fighting and yelling got so bad that Jane ran to the elderly neighbor's condo. She was having pains and slight bleeding. She thought she might be miscarrying. Against her wishes, the neighbor called an ambulance and decided to go to the hospital with her. Meanwhile, Bob was out of control. He continued to threaten Jane and their neighbor. They requested a police escort.

Upon their arrival, Jane was rushed into the examination room as her neighbor reported to the police and the doctors what happened. They were able to save the baby from premature birth but Jane remained in the hospital for several days. Her neighbor called her parents who rushed to be with her. They took her home with them and several months later she delivered a beautiful baby girl. She negotiated through her lawyers to drop all charges against her now ex-husband if he would sign away all parental rights and never contact them again. He agreed.

Fourteen years later, Jane met and fell in love with her daughter's soccer coach. They're happily married and her former neighbor is their daughter's godmother.

The End

We find one compassionate person who is willing to step up to the plate and help someone they don't know in both stories. I think about the many times I have thought a situation was none of my business. I clearly remember a time when I pulled up into a shopping center and parked beside a car with a family inside of it. The male was punching a young male child sitting in the back seat with his fists. A female was holding an infant in her arms and staring straight ahead. She looked pained but never uttered a word. My first reaction was disbelief and then anger. My next thought was I have to say or do something. I put my hand on my door handle but fear rose up and I didn't move. The male turned back around in the driver's seat and drove off. I felt ashamed and saddened for several hours. There are ways that we can help someone in distress without endangering our lives. I think of the compassion of Jesus when we have been beaten down, battered and bruised by life. He almost always provides a means of escape for us.

Prayer

Father, help us to have the compassion and the courage to help others as needed. Create in us a clean heart and renew the right spirit. We're grateful that You showed us mercy in our time of need. Thank You, Lord. Amen

Healing Prompt

Purpose in your heart to do unto others as you would have them do unto you. Ask the Lord to give you compassion and the gift of mercy to be able to help others.

The Parable of the Talent

Matthew 25:14-18

[14] For the kingdom of heaven is as a man traveling into a far country, who called his own servants, and delivered unto them his goods. [15] And unto one he gave five talents, to another two, and to another one; to every man according to his several ability; and straightway took his journey. [16] Then he that had received the five talents went and traded with the same, and made them other five talents. [17] And likewise he that had received two, he also gained other two.[18] But he that had received one went and digged in the earth, and hid his lord's money.

This story is told by Jesus to His disciples as an example of what God expects of kingdom citizens. We have all been given what we need to fulfill our purpose in life. Everyone used what their master gave them except the servant with one talent. He buried it to his detriment. Jesus commended the faithful servants who were wise stewards but took the talent from the unwise servant and gave it to the one with five talents, which confirms the word of to whom much is given, much is required.

MY VERSION

Parable of the Talents

Once upon a time, there were five servants who were given gifts and talents. One was a loving wife and mother who started a home daycare and was able to enhance the lives of many children. She and her husband eventually fostered kids. It wasn't an easy thing to do because they also had biological kids. Nevertheless, they knew that they had something to offer the foster kids. They did this for years until one year they decided to add to their family by the process of adoption. It wasn't an easy process, but with love and determination, they were able to do it. She, therefore, doubled the talent and gift she was entrusted with.

The second servant was a giver. She helped others in their times of need by sharing food, cars or money. She allowed others to live with her when they didn't have a place to stay. She bought extra groceries so she could share. She supported youth activities in her church with financial donations. She started a non-profit organization that helped low-income families with children. She graciously used her talent and gift to help others.

The third servant loved to cook for others. She was often called to share in this capacity. She looked for ways to be a blessing to others. Sometimes she would carry fresh vegetables and other items to those in need. She would also transport the elderly to church on most Sundays. She shared her testimony of abundant blessings after a life of struggle. She influenced many who needed encouragement or a helping hand. She used her gift and talent wisely.

The fourth servant loved to document family history and share her knowledge with others. She was a hard worker, who loved her family and always enjoyed lively conversations with them. She diligently gathered photos and followed birthdays, weddings and funeral dates. You could always count on her to share facts about past family history. Her gift and talent were useful when some family members wanted to conduct a genealogy search. She was dedicated to using the knowledge she acquired.

The fifth servant was talented in several areas. She would start projects and never complete them. She would have great ideas but procrastinated with implementing them. She never seemed motivated to use the gifts and talents that were given to her. It made her sad until she realized she would waste what she was entrusted with if she didn't use her gifts. So, she followed through and began to excel in whatever she applied herself to.

The End

I feel eternally grateful when I reflect on the gifts and talents that God has entrusted me with. I'm grateful because I feel as if it took me a longer time than most to discover them. I was in church one Sunday during praise and worship and my husband was running across the floor, praising the Lord when I heard that still small voice of the Lord saying, "you need to run behind him because you have a lot of catching up to do. I have prepared many things for both of you."

I knew that the Lord was exhorting me to yield quicker to His spiritual prompting because He'd previously dealt with me about having strong self-will. I pray for the wisdom of God daily that I may find myself in His perfect will. I know God as a redeemer of time, because He propelled me through open doors, divine relationships and endless spiritual exploits. I want to use my gifts and talents for the work of the kingdom and for the glory of God. I truly want to hear "well done, thou good and faithful servant: thou hast been faithful over a few things, I will make thee ruler over many things: enter thou into the joy of thy lord (Matt. 25:21).

If you want to enter into joy, I challenge you to treasure the gift of God that you are. There is something inside of you that'll most certainly be a blessing to someone on this earth. We were created to show forth the glory of God, who is the creator of all things. He knows everything about you. He knows your struggles, failures, and mistakes, but the story doesn't end there. He also knows your triumphs, successes, and victories. I also encourage you to seek out and stir up your spiritual gifts.

The only way to access your spiritual gifts is by having the spirit of Christ living inside of you. The Apostle Paul earnestly pleaded with the disciples to walk worthy of their call. He knew that along with the call, came a grace to fully live out the purpose for which they were called. The Bible says we have been called out of darkness into the marvelous light that we may show forth the praises of God (1 Pet. 2:9). He called us on purpose. I encourage you to walk in purpose, live on purpose and allow the Lord to be glorified in you (Eph. 4:1, 7).

Prayer

Father, I thank You for Your great love towards us. I also thank You for the gifts that You have freely bestowed upon us. We desire to please You in every aspect of our lives. Give us wisdom, understanding, and knowledge to fulfill the call on our lives. Amen.

Healing Prompt

Appreciate the grace of God and share His love with others.

EPILOGUE

2 Corinthians 3:2-3

² Ye are our epistle written in our hearts, known and read of all men:³ Forasmuch as ye are manifestly declared to be the epistle of Christ ministered by us, written not with ink, but with the Spirit of the living God; not in tables of stone, but in fleshy tables of the heart.

The Lord posed a question to me in the process of completing this book. He asked, "if you were a living epistle that'll be read by men, how would you like to be known?" I'd never had that particular question posed to me before so I was somewhat surprised. I couldn't give an immediate answer. I pondered it for several days. I asked a question of my own: "since you know my heart Lord, how will I be known?" I didn't receive an answer. I continued each day to ponder the question in my heart and here is my answer:

If I were an epistle (letter), I would almost certainly want to be a love letter. I would want mankind to know that the greatest love imaginable came in the person of Jesus Christ and totally transformed my life. He has written pages in my heart of deliverance, emotional healings, and unspeakable joy. The Lord, through the person and work of the Holy Spirit, has saturated me with His agape love until it has permeated my very being. I now love others as I have never been able to love before. I know that it is a supernatural love. I can't describe the love of God that is written upon my heart, so I direct you to the scriptures that were inspired by the Creator. I read First Corinthians chapter thirteen and found that I wanted to be read as a verse four Christian.

1 Corinthians 13:1-13 NIV

¹If I speak in the tongues of men or of angels, but do not have love, I am only a resounding gong or a clanging cymbal. ² If I have the gift of prophecy and can fathom all mysteries and all knowledge, and if I have a faith that can move mountains, but do not have love, I am nothing. ³ If I give all I possess to the poor and give over my body to hardship that I may boast, but do not have love, I gain nothing. ⁴ Love is patient, love is kind. It does not envy, it does not boast, it is not proud. ⁵ It does not dishonor others, it is not self-seeking, it is not easily angered, it keeps no record of wrongs. ⁶ Love does not delight in evil but rejoices with the truth. ⁷ It always protects, always trusts, always hopes, always perseveres. ⁸ Love never fails. But where there are prophecies, they will cease; where there are tongues, they will be stilled; where there is knowledge, it will pass away. ⁹ For we know in part and we prophesy in part, ¹⁰ but when completeness comes, what is in part disappears. ¹¹ When I was a child, I talked like a child, I thought like a child, I reasoned like a child. When I became a man, I put the ways of childhood behind me. ¹² For now, we see only a reflection as in a mirror; then we shall see face to face. Now I know in part; then I shall know fully, even as I am fully known. ¹³ And now these three remain faith, hope, and love. But the greatest of these is love.

So, I would like to reiterate that if I were a living epistle, love would be highlighted on each page.

Dear readers,

I want to share a few words with you who love to read as I do. I want to share what freedom feels like to me. Freedom is laying my head on a pillow to sleep instead of putting a pillow over my head to drown out the noise of yelling, fighting, cursing and constant arguments. Freedom is reading and reading and reading until my heart's content. Freedom is buying books because I can. Freedom is knowing that if I can't find the book that I'm looking for, I have the capability to write it myself. Freedom is knowing that I'm no longer an ugly duckling but a beautiful swan.

My Prayer

Father, I'm so grateful that I've experienced Your love and mercy before I transitioned from this earth. You have transformed my life and I know that You make everything beautiful in its time. I pray for every reader of this book: Grant them the time to experience Your unfailing love, tender mercies and grace. Bless them with the spiritual blessings that are in heavenly places. Bring healing and freedom in every area of their lives. I pray this in the matchless name of Jesus. Amen

Love,
Juliette

NOTES

Fairy Tales;
"Literary Terms." Literary Terms. 1 June 2015. Web. 3 Nov. 2016.
<https://literaryterms.net/>.

Fantasy Tales;
https://www.dictionary.com/browse/fantasy

Made in the USA
Middletown, DE
09 June 2020

96928121R00092